MORE PRAISE FOR
## *ALWAYS CRASHING IN THE SAME CAR:*
## *A NOVEL AFTER DAVID BOWIE*

"Already the author of among the most distinguished bodies
of work in contemporary American letters, one that includes
marvels like *Girl Imagined by Chance*, *Dreamlives of Debris*, and
*My Red Heaven*, Lance Olsen outdoes himself with *Always
Crashing in the Same Car*. As he takes us on a moving, multinod-
al journey through the stunning kaleidoscope that was David
Bowie's life, Olsen offers up a generous vision of the indispens-
able role of art, love, and friendship as—with old mortality
in the offing—we prosecute the wonders of our days and the
challenges of our nights."

> —**Laird Hunt**, author of *The Impossibly*

"Lance Olsen concocts a world in which the concoction of
self is spectacularly illegible and gorgeously weird. Biography,
lit crit, metafiction, history: everything and nothing belongs.
Time is confetti and here comes the wind. Love and father-
hood, fortune and fame. Augury, memory, dream. Nothing's
sortable. This book blew my mind—it's all questions, super-
charged and divine."

> —**Noy Holland**, author of *I Was Trying to Describe
> What It Feels Like*

"Bewildered and bereft, adrift in the ever-grief of his wife's
death, scholar Alec Nolens seeks comfort by immersing himself in the sea of words surrounding David Bowie, a project
he imagines as a 'love song,' not so much to Bowie, 'as to the
lacunae around the thought of him.' Lance Olsen's visionary

novel is the apotheosis of such a project. *Always Crashing in the Same Car* offers a kaleidoscope of Davids tenderly dissolving into Davy Jones, a desperately human human being awakened to the expansive possibilities of consciousness by the news of his own impending departure, an un-Bowied genius composing his own rapturous elegy to this transient interlude we call a life."

—**Melanie Rae Thon**, author of *As If Fire Could Hide Us*
and *The Voice of the River*

"*Always Crashing in the Same Car* presents a phantasmagorical mosaic of facts and fantasies concerning the life and art of David Bowie, for whom the mask always melted into the face and vice versa. A meditation on memory, loss, and love; on the projection of a writer's self through their chosen idols; on the artist's attempt to orchestrate the manner of a life's conclusion. All this, Lance Olsen delivers, and more."

—**Jonathan Lethem**, author of *The Fortress of Solitude*

"In *Always Crashing in the Same Car*, David Bowie woos Iman with tales of the Museum of Jurassic Technology, that wonder-cabinet of the lurid imaginary. So, too, Lance Olsen's novel, which presents Bowie as *Citizen Kane*, as the Dylan of *I'm Not There*, as that lyric which won't parse, that image which becomes iconic but can't simply communicate. Olsen ellipsizes a greedy-yet-giving Bowie, reader as much as rocker, neither celebrated nor reviled—Davy, determined to never be Mr. Jones."

—**Eric Weisbard**, author of *Songbooks:
The Literature of American Popular Music*

# ALWAYS
# CRASHING
# IN THE
# SAME CAR

# ALSO BY LANCE OLSEN

# ALWAYS CRASHING IN THE SAME CAR

### A Novel after David Bowie

# LANCE OLSEN

TUSCALOOSA

FC2 is an imprint of the University of Alabama Press

Inquiries about reproducing material from this work should be addressed
to the University of Alabama Press

Book Design: Publications Unit, Department of English, Illinois State
    University; Director: Steve Halle, Production Intern: Brooke Novie
Cover design: Matthew Revert
Typeface: Baskerville URW

Library of Congress Cataloging-in-Publication Data is available from
the Library of Congress.

ISBN (paper): 978-1-57366-199-7
ISBN (e-book): 978-1-57366-901-6

for Andi,
as long as there's sun

Jasmine, I saw you peeping
As I pushed my foot down to the floor
I was going round and round the hotel garage
Must have been touching close to ninety-four
Oh, but I'm always crashing in the same car
—David Bowie

You know, don't you, that God is a bookseller? He published one book—the text of suffering—over and over again. He disguises it between new boards, in different shapes and sizes, prints on varying papers, in many fonts, adds prefaces and postscripts to deceive the buyer, but it's always the same book.

—John Edgar Wideman

**OH YOU PRETTY THINGS**

Humming something that came to him in red dreams, he considers, mid-shave, this man suddenly in his late sixties, this man who looks fifteen years younger than he is—he considers mid-shave the anomaly situated on his jawline just in front of his right earlobe.

How he never noticed it before he took this breath this morning, not even six o'clock yet, his wife asleep a little longer, quick white spring light after last night's rain rushing every surface in the bathroom.

How time has unexpectedly and irreversibly arisen in that tiny corner of him when he wasn't being anyone.

The bluegreen smudge, the deviation, no larger than a five-point $o$ in Baskerville typeface. He considers it, and somewhere inside the next breath forgets it, this burl of self-awareness unsettling into eagerness for his first cup of coffee, his first cigarette of three or four packs today, the pleasant understated shocks of them.

The book he will slip into by the incandescent wall of living room windows.

All the silences he will find in it.

All the noise.

## SOUND + VISION

*The sound of a truck at fifty miles per hour,* the man is reading, stretched out on the cream-colored leather couch in that sunshine squall, having remembered as he moved toward it, coffee cup in hand, the daily letdown: he no longer smokes.

He hasn't smoked for years.

Not since—how can his body forget something like that?

*Static between stations. Rain. We want to capture and control these sounds, to use them not as sound effects but as musical instruments.*

An almost perfectly square black first edition of John Cage's first volume, a collection of lectures and essays published when he was already forty-nine, still not quite John Cage, in 1961, Wesleyan University Press, mint condition, which the man stumbled across yesterday browsing the rat's nest of stacks at the Strand, no ambition except to see where the shelves led him after lunch, his favorite, a bagged chicken sandwich with watercress and tomatoes from Olive's on Prince Street eaten on a bench in Washington Square, listening to shih tzus and squirrels squabbling, kids skateboarding, someone playing jazz, unimprovised Keith Jarrett, on an upright piano the pianist wheeled in from somewhere all the way to the fountain.

He first read this book—when did he first read it?

The early seventies, he would guess, though he can't recall with any certainty. The only way the man knows for sure he read it is because he read about himself reading it in a biography about him. He reads every one of them, even his ex's, even Angie's, his little darling blowtorch, ever fascinated, ever puzzled, about how others write him into themselves.

At the time, Ziggy Stardust had abridged his diet to the elemental: cocaine, milk, red peppers, and Angie's rage. At the time, Ziggy Stardust, the bisexual alien rock star who attained fame only as earth unraveled into its final five years, couldn't tell anyone anymore who Ziggy Stardust really was because he was no longer anything except this burst of coked-up energy and anxiety and immortality, and next he had to get out of Britain.

He had to get out of Los Angeles.

He had to reach grimy gray walled-in Berlin to slip the habit and slip Angie and reawaken his music within Brian Eno's gravitational vehemences.

*Given four phonographs*, the man reads, *we can compose and perform a quartet for explosive motor, wind, heartbeat, and landslide.*

Did he ever encounter that line before?

Once upon a time Cage's words reconfigured him, yet he can't remember any of them. Not with anything like specificity. They lived inside him for more than a quarter century, operating softly, unremittingly, and nowhere except on the page in front of him right now for the first time.

You read a book with this belief that you will never leave it behind, yet twenty pages in you can't summon a single detail from page three. The event begins dissolving as if on some dimmer switch. One month, two years, and, if you're lucky, you're still sustaining a gauzy set of emotions about it, a couple out-of-focus images, maybe a loose idea, this rattling tin box of character traits.

If you're lucky.

If you're not, maybe it's only a half-recollected title swelling out of addle, an author's name, this spreading unease in the face of what books actually are all about at the end of the day: memory's fiasco.

Lying on the couch, it comes to him that, if every cell composing a person resurrects every seven or ten years, then this man in his late sixties, listening to the sounds of his wife stirring into her day in the kitchen, has been an absolute somebody else at least three times since first reading the lines he can't be one hundred percent convinced he has ever read, and yet can, and yet can't.

**ALL THE YOUNG DUDES**

That interviewer asking you when you were in your forties what you would like your legacy to look like, and you answering: *I'd love people to believe I had really great haircuts.*

In 2018, two years after your death, the first statue in your honor unveiled in Market Square, Aylesbury, Buckinghamshire, about an hour-and-a-half drive northwest of London: a hideous bronze likeness of you from 2002—the year *Heathen* appeared, two years before the first of your six heart attacks—*six*—casting an amused eye at your alter egos spilling out before you, in the forefront a Ziggy with a monstrous grouper mouth looking nothing at all like Ziggy, while speakers mounted above play one of your songs every hour. The night after its reveal, someone spray-paints across the base: *Feed the homeless first.*

Your mother, Peggy, a cinema usherette. In every photo she puts up with, she wears a grimace, as if physically pained to be where and who she is. And there you are, always smiling stoically beside her, your need for her attention, to broach and traverse her emotional death strip, palpable.

How you intuit that, for young people with difficulty forming, your formlessness tells them it's okay to be lost. cf. Major Tom.

Among your favorite artists: Tintoretto, Erich Heckel, Picasso—the first for his bold brushwork, furious energy, and dramatic gestures; the second for his rough, spontaneous marks and vivid flat color in those angular, expressionist woodcuts; the third for his tireless curiosity and refusal to roost.

Journalists noting you change your accent depending on who is in a room with you.

5

Your first auditory love: Little Richard. *Without him*, you telling another interviewer, *half of my contemporaries and I wouldn't be playing music.*

You never seem to get old, not in any sense that matters.

And yet.

Five feet, ten inches tall, you certainly never seem old enough to die.

Eleven, you perform makeshift dances to records by Bill Haley, Fats Domino, and Elvis Presley by yourself in your bedroom and before your parents' friends on Christmas Eve.

Your father, John, a promotions officer for Dr. Barnardo's charity, which has provided shelter for homeless children since the 1870s.

You noting: Elvis Aaron Presley: January 8, 1935.

You noting: David Robert Jones: January 8, 1947.

Journalists noting you answer their questions in a way that gives them what they want to hear rather than what you necessarily believe.

You knew they didn't believe you, so you knew you could tell them the truth.

"Space Oddity," whose title puns on Stanley Kubrick's 1968 film, *2001: A Space Odyssey*, is perhaps not so accidentally released on July 11, 1969, five days before Apollo 11 lifts off for the moon and nine before the BBC plays it during coverage of the landing, thereby begetting your first big hit (fourteen weeks on the British charts; top position: number five) and, after nearly a decade of musical flounders, finally getting your career off the ground.

Throughout your life, you feel a connection with cultural refugees trying to attain escape velocity.

*Tomorrow*, you telling another interviewer, *belongs to those who can hear it coming.*

Born in Brixton, seven hundred yards from Her Majesty's Prison.

You hate tea; love Oasis, Placebo, and Arcade Fire during your last years; are innately both "masculine" and "feminine" (our cautious culture's joke categories), yet neither; arch, clownish, clever, dry, emotionally remote; alternately contemplative, vain, kind, collaborative in spirit, a consummate flatterer, sincerely charming—yet you can turn off that charm like a slamming door if you see you're not getting your way.

Your laugh: explosive.

John Major, Prime Minister and leader of the Conservative Party from 1990 to 1997, traversing his youth several streets over from you. His father: acrobat and juggler, naturally.

As his psychedelic astronaut, Major Tom, floats helplessly into outer space, Camille Paglia observing, we sense that the sixties counterculture has transmuted into a hopelessness about political reform.

Your lyrics: cryptic, jagged, sometimes the product of Burroughs-esque cut-up, without fail ironic, studied, tonally off-kilter.

Early on, confusing you with your role as the leper messiah, fans want to touch you, hold you close, be assured someone understands and cares about them, absorb your life force—but at the deepest level you don't care about them, only the heat of their adoration, regard them with suspicion, even as you let them do what they need to do, because that allows you to do what you need to do.

*Till there was rock*, you sing in "Sweet Head," an outtake from *The Rise and Fall of Ziggy Stardust, you only had God.*

You like to emphasize for effect that as a boy you walked to school past V-2 bomb sites, without, however, pointing out this is true of almost all children in London throughout the years immediately following the war.

To thank him for the piece he wrote about you in *Rolling Stone* in the early nineties, you send journalist David Wild a pig fetus in a jar.

Fifty, you tell a reporter: *I cannot express to younger people how great it is to be this age. It's like describing the taste of a peach. They'll find out when they get here.*

How you adored your half brother Terry. Nine years older than you, apotheosis of cool, he introduces you to Kerouac's *On the Road*, Buddhism, and Coltrane. In his twenties, Terry develops schizophrenia and spends much of the rest of his life in and out of institutions. One snowy morning in January 1985, age forty-eight, he strolls off the grounds of the Cane Hill Mental Hospital, crosses the road to the train station, and ambles down to the southern end of the platform. Seeing the express train appear in the distance, he jumps onto the tracks, lays his head upon the rail, and turns his face away from the future.

You receive your first instruments as presents before you are ten: a plastic saxophone, a tin guitar, a xylophone.

An asteroid, formerly known as 2008 YN3, is renamed 342843 Davidbowie in your honor days before your sixty-eighth birthday.

At the height of your drug years (*I like fast drugs*, you telling yet another interviewer. *I hate anything that slows me down.*), you become frantically paranoid, for a time keeping your urine in your refrigerator, believing that way no wizard can use it to enchant you.

When you are twenty-three, you forming the Hype and cajoling everyone in your band to dress up as superheroes. Everywhere you play, you are booed off stage.

Over the course of your career, you record four hundred songs and sell one hundred forty million albums.

*Fame,* you say to a journalist, *can take interesting men and thrust mediocrity upon them.*

Predictably, almost parodically, you underperform at school, leaving in 1963 with only one qualification, a basic O level— an Ordinary—in art.

Among your school friends: Peter Frampton, whose father is your art instructor. You and Peter stay in touch, even play together on and off, throughout your life.

Your imagination: omniphagic, ingesting anything in any medium that spawns and/or helps spawn your visions.

*I was a Buddhist on Tuesday and I was into Nietzsche by Friday,* you telling yet another interviewer. *Most of my life has been like that.*

Your aunt Vivienne: also diagnosed with schizophrenia. Your aunt Una: dies in her late thirties after spending years in and out of mental institutions, receiving a number of rounds of electroconvulsive therapy along the way. Your aunt Nora: a lobotomy because, declares the report, she has a case of *bad nerves*.

Among your teen friends: Reginald Kenneth Dwight, briefly, before gestating into Elton John. As your reputations snowball, your friendship melts away into petty resentments.

Scientists name a large electric-yellow spider from Southeast Asia after you eight years before you are cremated secretly in New Jersey for $700, sans funeral, sans family or friends, your ashes later scattered on Bali: *Heteropoda davidbowie*.

cf. Major Tom in particular and outer space in general as your signature metaphors, not for freedom and possibility, as one might guess, but rather for existential estrangement, loneliness, contingency, the bottomless dread of drift: "Ashes to Ashes," "Moonage Daydream," "Starman," "Life on Mars?," "Dancing Out in Space," "Born in a UFO," "Lazarus," "Blackstar," und so weiter.

Intractably uninterested in formal education, a model autodidact, you always prefer teaching yourself to being taught, whatever that means. Filming Nicolas Roeg's *The Man Who Fell to Earth* in New Mexico in 1975, you have become a twenty-eight-year-old cocaine addict weighing ninety-five pounds. You refuse to travel by plane, positive most flights end in flames, so you show up in July by train—along with three specially designed steamer trunks that open out to display neatly the fifteen-hundred volumes that make up your mobile library. Between shoots you disappear into your trailer to try to swim back toward sobriety by reading.

Ten years earlier, you change your name from David Jones to David Bowie because Davy Jones of the Monkees has become vastly more popular than you. The intended connotation: the famous knife, cutting through all the fatty lies termed civilization.

Contrary to the myth, you don't evince heterochromia, wherein an individual's eyes are two different colors, blue and brown in your case, but rather anisocoria, wherein one pupil is larger than the other, in your case your left than your right—this because your friend George Underwood punches you in January 1962 during a fight over a girl at school, resulting in a deep corneal abrasion, paralysis of your left iris's sphincter, and four months' hospital treatment. You never again see clearly out of that eye, permanently suffer poor depth perception.

Fifty-one years later, Canadian astronaut Chris Hadfield records a tribute version of "Space Oddity," strumming on his acoustic guitar as he floats through the International Space Station.

*The measure of Bowie's success,* Mikal Gilmore summarizes in *Rolling Stone* four years before your death, *isn't whether or not he could remake himself and move on. The measure is that he helped others to proclaim identities that they had once been shamed, or intimidated, into denying.*

Angie dreams up holy gestures for you—e.g., you extending a pleading hand to the audience while performing "Rock 'n' Roll Suicide"—thereby amping up your role as Savior Machine, Sacrifice Engine. In Floria Sigismondi's video for "The Next Day," criticized by the Catholic church (Gary Oldman: horny priest; Marion Cotillard: weary prostitute spurting stigmata in an S&M brothel called the Decameron), you pose as Christ who, in a wink at the end, ascends to heaven, or at least out of the picture. While organized religion may be on the decline, reviewers point out, the sacred is alive, well, and grotesque.

At the time of your death, your net worth is, give or take a few, one hundred million dollars. You leave half, as well as your SoHo apartment, to your wife Iman. Twenty-five percent goes to Duncan, your son by Angie. Your daughter by Iman, Alexandria—Lexi—receives twenty-five percent, in addition to the family's upstate New York property near Woodstock, Little Tonche Mountain, sixty-four acres in the middle of which lies a country retreat with positively sensational views.

In 1985 a publisher asks Jorge Luis Borges to choose his hundred favorite books and write an introduction to each. Borges only gets to number seventy-four before he moves to the wrong side of the grass. In preparation for the March 2014 opening of the *David Bowie Is . . .* retrospective at The Victoria and Albert Museum, you put together and publish a list of the hundred books you feel have most influenced you, in part an homage to Borges.

Number one on Borges's list is Julio Cortázar's stories, numbers two and three the apocryphal gospels, number four *Amerika* and *The Complete Stories of Kafka*. Number one on your list is Anthony Burgess's novel about violence in extremis, *A Clockwork Orange*, without which there would be no Ziggy Stardust, who at the beginning of his concerts struts onto the stage accompanied by Beethoven's Symphony No. 9 rendered via Moog synthesizer, a salute to Alex DeLarge and his Droogs, while the Spiders from Mars sport costumes modeled on those from Stanley Kubrick's 1971 adaptation of Burgess's 1962 dystopia.

By the time you are twenty-eight, you play: guitar, alto and tenor sax, piano, mellotron, Moog, harmonica, mouth harp, koto, mandolin, recorder, viola, violin, cello, and the stylophone—competently, but never with anything even close to mastery.

*Yes, of course I'm gay, and always have been,* you confessing to *Melody Maker's* Michael Watts in 1972, even as you concurrently assured your mother on the phone: *Don't believe a word of it, mum.*

Homosexuality having been decriminalized in Britain only five years before.

From your liner notes on *Outside: All art is unstable. . . . There is no authoritative voice, there are only multiple readings.*

There unfold 4.3 million tweets about you within twenty-four hours of your departure.

*Don't you love the* Oxford Dictionary*?* you telling a broadcaster. *When I first read it, I thought it was a really, really long poem about everything.*

On *Diamond Dogs*, the story goes, you play nearly every instrument.

*There's a sense that I know where I am now*, you explaining to a columnist. *I recognize life and most of its experiences, and I'm quite comfortable with the idea of the finality of it. But it doesn't stop me trying to continually resolve it: resolve the questions about it. I think I'll still be doing it—hopefully—like Strauss at eighty-four.*

Postmortem, astronomers name an asterism—a prominent pattern of stars smaller than a constellation—after you: seven present near Mars at the moment of your death that, seen just right, form the lightning-bolt constellation reminiscent of your Aladdin Sane face paint.

Number two on your list: Camus's *The Stranger*; number three: Nik Cohn's *Awopbopaloobop Alopbamboom*, arguably the first serious, extended critical work about pop music, with an emphasis on 1968, the year the Beatles' *White Album* and Stones' *Beggars Banquet* were released.

In typography, an asterism refers to a typographic symbol consisting of three asterisks placed in a triangle. It is used to indicate minor breaks in text, call attention to a passage, or separate subchapters in a book.

*Before the internet*, music journalist Paul Morley commenting, *you being a one-man Google search engine.*

Doctors incorrectly diagnose Anthony Burgess with terminal brain cancer. His reaction: write five novels as quickly as possible in order to support his soon-to-be widow. *A Clockwork Orange* takes him three weeks. Its inspiration: his first wife's—Lynne's—assault in 1944 during a London blackout by a group of American soldiers out for a little fun. Pregnant, she miscarries.

The name you and Iman use signing into hotels: *Mr. and Ms. Anthrope.*

*I change my mind a lot*, you mentioning to a commentator. *I usually don't agree with what I say very much.*

During your LA years, you begin wearing a cross. You never take it off.

Iman bears a bowie knife tattooed on her ankle, around her belly button the Arabic lettering for *David.*

*When I first went back to have a look at the World Trade Center area after 9/11,* you telling yet another interviewer, *I thought, my god, it looks like London East End, you know, when I was a kid. It's what it looked like when I was about seven. It brought it all back.* The viable implication—that you had an especially rough childhood in an especially bleak part of the city—is a gentle distortion you liked to perpetuate, according to your biographer Wendy Leigh, who explains you *grew up petted and privileged,* not *a working-class hero by any stretch.* Six, you moved from Brixton to Bromley in Kent, hardly an impoverished London neighborhood. The persona you fostered to the contrary, you were a suburban kid who wanted to duck out of the lethal blandness ASAP. You felt like an outsider there, just like every teen does everywhere.

Dylan Jones, another of your biographers, recounts his father once asking him what he was working on.

Jones responded he was writing a book about your remarkable appearance on *Top of the Pops* on that Thursday evening in July 1972 when you sang "Starman" for the first time, blowing away viewers across the UK. Jones will use those three minutes and thirty-three seconds, the precise instant your name went aboveground and nationwide, he explained, to explore how you influenced an entire generation of music and fashion.

His father hesitated, then asked Jones why.

*I reeled off the various elements of his performance that had been so challenging, so inspiring, and so transgressive,* Jones writes. *I described the way in which Bowie had toyed sexually with his guitarist Mick Ronson, the way in which he had dressed like a pansexual spaceman, the way he sashayed across the screen like a 1920s film star, and, saliently, the way in which his flame-red hair, his Day-Glo jumpsuit, and the general glam color fest had almost colonized the program. I explained that this was the moment when the seventies finally outgrew the sixties, when the monochrome world of boring, boring southeast England had exploded in a fiesta of color.*

*My father looked at the floor, took a moment, and then said, very quietly: You know we had a black-and-white television, don't you?*

## LIFE ON MARS

—scribbles Alec Nolens on another index card, I scribble, on the third day of his third sabbatical, mine, which we envision as a yearlong series of experiments in thinking, empathy, and doubt. Still bleary from the transatlantic flight, I am sitting at the desk in the bedroom of a third-floor apartment in a leafy, cobblestoned neighborhood of Berlin three thousand nine hundred and sixty-five miles away from where you left nearly a decade ago, pile of those cards already having propagated beside me and my proliferating pile of biographies, interviews, critical studies, and photo albums, four boxes of them shipped ahead so they'd be waiting for me here at the corner of Prenzlauer Allee and Wörther Straße.

It is reckless May-morning bird gibber in the courtyard trees outside my cracked-open window.

It is me sipping coffee while watching David Bowie try to gather before me, break up, disperse, try to gather again.

This is a form of happiness, these askings, these attempts at understanding what one can't understand. That's why we read, I'm coming to reckon. That's why we write. For those silvery flashes, not of figuring it out, but of revisiting the act of unlearning, the giddy scramble of uncertainty at the back of the brainpan.

That's why this project will be a love song, not so much to him, as to the lacunae around the thought of him, the idea of caesura as a marker for moving through the world, directions for a kind of life dance, let's call it, because that's what's left us when everything is said and done.

Isn't it?

That, and a love song to the part of his life, anyone's, almost nobody talks about, noisy spectacle habitually catching the ear and interest long before something like muted equipoise and insight does: those later years we will enter, if things go extremely well, during which the ordinary, the internal, the gently baffled start to overtake the jangle and glare of our formerly operatic first-persons.

What ensues after you've stepped off the stage at *Top of the Pops*, set the city on fire, and next it's who cares and that was someone else decades back.

When you arrive at a point in your life where instructions for being a rock star are hereafter lacking.

When, now fifty-five, you find yourself divided from yourself, telling yet another interviewer: *I never became who I should have been until maybe twelve or fifteen years ago.*

And who was that?

Who knows?

You don't. I don't. Surely no so-called aficionado does. Aficionados undoubtedly know the least of anyone about their subject because they believe they know the most. That's the point. I'm coming to conclude the world boils down to reading. People pick up books looking for what they think books will eternally supply: a *because*. Before long, if they're not vigilant, they start reading other people as if they were books. That's where everything goes wrong. Read anyone closely enough, and the *because* fades out like the last refrain of a pop song.


In his study of Dostoevsky, ever creaked out in grad programs' rusty critical wheelbarrow, there's a niche nobody remembers because they're busy droning on about platitudes concerning dialogism (beginning on page fifty-three, in case you'd like to have a look; University of Minnesota Press, 1984; trans. Caryl Emerson), when Mikhail Bakhtin discusses the notion of unfinalizability.

The only moment, he says, any of us can be defined—and then only partially, fleetingly, failingly—is when we're dead, which is to say when we have ceased changing, which is to say ceased being alive. All the other minutes of us are unclosed and indeterminate. Our consciousnesses can never be thoroughly contained by others' calcifications.

Or our own.

Period.

Expand from individual to existential, and you get: *Nothing conclusive has yet taken place in the world, the ultimate word of the world and about the world has not yet been spoken, the world is open and free, everything is still in the future and will always be in the future.*

So it is with the book in your lap. You can never stop reading it, once you've commenced, not for the rest of your life, despite shaky indications to the contrary.

Books provide us with the pretense of making sense of things (every form suggests a philosophy), but the things they make sense of are constructions inhabited by fictions with crafted intensions, all loose ends interlaced and cinched. Each time we return to a text, regardless of our best efforts, the years will have regenerated it, our sublet world become reorganized around it, we will have been translated into another foreign tongue of ourselves.

That's really why books are so dangerous: not—or not only—that they introduce us to concepts that are deliriously new and unnerving (we fear what we cannot solve, even as we relish it), but that they seem to make sense of other people's lives, never our own, because *because* is a category of grammatical mistake that exposes something vastly more troublesome than the two syllables, four vowels, and three consonants which encompass it.

That's the point. Some people as they age settle into stubborn conviction resembling conclusive vision. When we're off our game, we sometimes refer to that as wisdom. Over the years, it appears those people have persuaded themselves of their own importance and perspicacity, finalized their own unfinalizability, notwithstanding reality.

Forgive me while I doze.

Other people: not so much so. Other people as they age displace into a fraught, breakable awareness of their own insignificance and contingency. Has there been a larger reason to me? To this deafening roar of time?

Is there a larger reason to reading Bowie? And, if so, has that larger reason come to seem meaningful simply because (have you noticed how grammar simply won't let you shake some words?) a certain number of people have judged a certain number of the faces he wore publicly for a few decades to be more compelling than those you and I have found ourselves wearing?

I wonder what the larger reason is to reading ourselves reading him—and then, mid-sentence, it occurs to me that's the wrong question to ask.

What's the right question?

Beats me.


I couldn't be more cognizant of the fact that I won't be writing many more books. There are only so many that living rewards you with, even if at the outset you don't have a clear sense of what that total might amount to.

Better be judicious.

Better pay attention.

Better keep an eye on the egg timer, or the years will bite you.

That didn't go well. Let me try again. There is this poem (trans. Clare Cavanagh) by the Polish poet Adam Zagajewski, which first appeared in the *New Yorker* on September 17, 2001, six days after 9/11, five years before Bowie's final public performance at New York's Hammerstein Ballroom (the last song he ever sang live: "Changes,"—anthem, obviously, to unfinalizability) on behalf of the Keep A Child Alive charity—there is this poem whose title and refrain consists of the line *praise the mutilated world.*

It asks us to think about ships setting out to sea, and how most of them will make it, but how a few won't. It asks us to think about how executioners sing beautiful songs as they work, and how there exist dazzling concerts and delicate light lost. It's enterprise of an older author, is my point, far beyond the existential reach of somebody who hasn't crested, say, his fifth decade, aware that every *hello* is invariably the first plosive of *goodbye.*

Not in any maudlin way.

Good god no.

There's nothing resigned about the realization, nothing in it that feels like surrender. It's just that if you read Zagajewski's poem attentively you'll notice there's not one single *because* in it.

That's all you need to know, really, to explain why this is the temporal sweep that interests me, the one more or less still taboo to bring up: What is it like to be the opposite of young? To care less and less about inexperience? To find the juvenile—with its chronic conviction that everything coming to pass before breakfast is equally, stupidly old—well, juvenile.

The essence of a human being, Gabriel García Márquez once commented, is resistant to the passage of time.

He's wrong.

It's not.

It most definitely, assuredly, is not.

Let me try again. "Where Are We Now?," the first single from Bowie's twenty-fourth studio album, *The Next Day*, was released via iTunes on January 8, 2013, Bowie's sixty-sixth birthday. It had been ten years since he had offered us any new music. On his website he posted an accompanying video by the kooky, poignant multimedia artist Tony Oursler. The video features Oursler's wife, Jacqueline Humphries, and Bowie as conjoined homunculi perched atop a pommel horse in Oursler's actual junk-stuffed New York studio, which Bowie frequented. Behind them on a screen runs grainy black-and-white footage from a grimy gray walled-in Berlin. To the left sits the model of a large blue ear, to the right one of a large white eye. We are in some fever-dream Wunderkammer that functions as stand-in for Bowie's imagination and remembrance.

This isn't a rock'n'roll suicide. This isn't a suffragette city. It's not Aladdin Sane or the Glass Spider or the Thin White Duke or the Man Who Fell to Earth, even if it is all about Heraclitus. Listen keenly, and you'll hear a voice washed through with time—frailer, more spectral, yearning, boundlessly more candid than its earlier iterations.

Maybe it's only a *performance* of sincerity, but I sincerely doubt it.

Listen, and you'll hear Bowie hanging out with Iggy Pop and Lou Reed at the club Dschungel in the seventies, throngs of East Germans passing over the Bösebrücke, first border crossing opened as the Wall fell on November 9, 1989—twenty thousand in the first hour alone, each unsure whether he or she was allowed to do what he or she was doing.

You'll hear Bowie's premier heart attack backstage during his June 25, 2004 performance at the Hurricane Festival in Scheeßel, Germany, his rush to emergency surgery for an acutely blocked artery.

What moves me most about it is how shot-through it is with an awareness of that blue-eyed boy Mr. Death leaning against the wall across the room, smiling without any lips, paring his fingernails, how it could never have been written by a musician in his forties or thirties, let alone his Stardust twenties.

That, after fifty, the face behind which you wear your faces becomes an exquisite, rending, unavoidable accomplishment.


## ZEROES

The motorcycle resuscitating beside him. The hydraulic hammer bang-bang-banging at some construction site down the block. Quick horn blats from the yellow cab over there, and then the one behind it, pursued by a general revving of motors.

The man mimics each sound under his breath, searching out the rhythmic continuities as he waits for the light to change at the corner of Lafayette and East Houston, air candy on his tongue, steps off the sidewalk amid a flock of pedestrians fluttering across the intersection, his thumb confirming the deviation in front of his right earlobe.

He could swear it feels larger than it did just a few hours ago.

Earlier, once Iman left to product select and organize a shoot at her company, he read.

She won't return until three-thirty or four.

Only now it is this FedEx truck backwards beeping.

It is this forced laughter of a teenage girl in an open furry pink ankle-length coat, white V-neck, and washed-out kneeless jeans idling with her friends on the median as he passes by.

Or is she shouting at them?

Arguing?

Crying?

Is that what she's doing?

Is this how sadness arrives today?

That must mean she loves someone.

The man read a while, then fooled around with the in-progress portrait on the easel he keeps beside the fireplace. The subject is somebody else, an ambulance driver on break he bumped into outside Ben's Pizzeria over on Prince, so he has titled it *Self-Portrait.*

He had to get out of Britain. He had to get out of Los Angeles. It felt like this other person was using his mind to think with and he wanted his thoughts back. And next he was recording at the Hansa Studios, a dreary, cavernous, repurposed

28

Weimar-era ballroom where the SS once held dances, where he could work on his music overlooking a no-man's-land patrolled by East German soldiers and those cemented-up windows in the apartment blocks on the far side and feel intoxicated and trapped and rediscover expressionism and let its jumpy distortions, ear-splitting colors, and blown-sideways perspective reanimate his own canvases.

He finds it difficult to design an answer when others ask him about his motivation. The satisfaction of doing a painting is never the satisfaction of doing a painting. The satisfaction is finishing the thing so he can move on to the next one. The process may be about the process, yet more it's somehow about getting through the process with one eye on what might come after.

He doesn't see any point to getting bogged down in the piece he's working with, all artsy and obsessive and immobilized. He can't understand artists and musicians who do. If something isn't going where it needs to go, why not drop it and wander somewhere else?

It's not particularly pleasant, this tackling a new painting, this making a new song.

That catches some people up short.

Artists like to say so, like to say it's the tackling that's the thing, but that's not right.

It's not enjoyment you feel. Enjoyment isn't even close to what you feel. It's something else.

It's—

That laugh-crying girl reminds him of someone from Berlin: his petite underfed German lover named—what was her name?

She was a little-needed time away from Romy Haag, the trans nightclub singer and dancer he fell in lust with at the start of his stay. Romy was like ushering a tornado into your subcutaneous tissue, everything and nothing in a whirlwind of splintered houses, an ongoing F5. But Katja—that's it: her name was Katja—Katja Kinder—he could encircle Katja's biceps with his thumb and forefinger, just like he could encircle his own back then.

Katja wore her black hair bobbed like women in the twenties, caked white makeup at twenty-two, chili-pepper-red lipstick. Every light in every niche of her had gone out, even as she pretended as hard as she could to be some species of optimist. She was never very good at it. He could always detect desperation in an optimist's voice. What Katja was good at was dodging her sorrow with counterfeit smiles and a meticulous system of reflexive evasion. Then she would slam into it all at once, full on, when her brakes let go. She was the kind of person who was going to be alone in life whether she was going to be alone in her life or not.

What he remembers most about their weeks as a couple in his Schöneberg flat above the auto-parts store is how Katja and he would spend whole days lying in bed, listening to Kraftwerk and Cluster, reading Dante's *Inferno* and Kafka's *Metamorphosis* to each other, drinking warm gin martinis, smoking Gitanes, talking about the future they knew they would never share, and crying together.

They liked being unbrave in each other's arms.

They could cry whole days away.

All the man could dream about were enormous bugs the size of babies flittering through his flat, dragging their insectile legs beneath them, he abiding in his nice white blousy dress, sailor's cap, and white high heels in the shadowy bedroom, watching them swarm.

A tenth of a second to parse and place a sound, that's all it takes the brain, and here there is a space-debris cloud of them: defunct launch vehicle stages, paint flecks, solidified liquids, bolts hurling twenty-two thousand miles an hour in perpetual orbit.

The sonic mess of an incessant car alarm.

The heavy breathing of a resting bus engine.

The rumble of the subway beneath your feet smashing through black.

A form of happiness, he wants to say as he moves up Mulberry, air sugary and spring-crisp after last night's rain, crowd dissipating behind him, all this restorative all-ness having nothing to do with him.

He has learned to turn anonymity on and off like his iPod playlist. It's easy here. That's what he adores about this city. Before, elsewhere, London, LA, it was the apprehension of constantly being seen. It was constantly being perceived as something not wholly human.

He became a sighting, a detection.

Here it's a flat lilac-gray cap, cheap shades, shabby lilac-gray hooded sweatshirt, tatty jeans, and who are you, and even if I knew I wouldn't give a shit.

It was John Lennon in house-husband mode wanting to show Sean the planet at the end of the seventies, inviting a group of his mates to meet up in Hong Kong for a week's holiday. Exploring the back streets one soggy afternoon, they heard a voice behind them. A cute kid, maybe ten or eleven, running up and asking, brisk with excitement: Are you John Lennon?

Without hesitation, John answered: No, but I wish I had his money.

Oh, sorry, said the kid, let down. Of course you're not.

And off he trotted.

A couple months later, out for a stroll through the Village, waiting for the light to change on the corner of Bleeker and MacDougal, the man heard this squeaky falsetto pipe up behind him: Are you David Bowie?

Without glancing back, he answered: No, but I wish I had his money.

You lying bastard, the voice replied. You wish you had *my* money.

He turned to discover John in a Mickey Mouse T-shirt, army pants, and combat boots.

There they both stood on that corner, John and Davy, ludicrously trying to unLennon and unBowie themselves, outdo each other's inconspicuousness as if the rest of New York hurrying around them didn't have better things to do than waste time recognizing them.


At Caffe Reggio the man likes the antique bench beneath the chiaroscuro painting aping a Caravaggio near the main window.

From there he can watch people passing by outside, study those jammed inside, the student in the eggplant NYU hoodie to his right reading what book is that, Baldwin, *God gave Noah the rainbow sign—no more water, the fire next time,* the green-haired emo in front of him endlessly picking pellets of snot from her nose, imagining herself for some reason unobserved, and there he is, nothing more than some guy in that flat lilac-gray cap among the clatter and chatter, jotting down a few ideas in his 3.5" x 5.5" Moleskine notebook.

Until Iman, until here, until the peace two people can enjoy together when it's their turn, his life never seemed entirely believable to him. In a way that thrilled him. In a way he relished finally reaching the far shore.

Now it is everything feels like Samuel Beckett's father's last words. Puttering around his house one day, he suffered a stroke, collapsed onto the floorboards, declared, staring up at the ceiling at a point far beyond his son's floating head, *What a morning*, and left himself.

Clear. Elementary. Attesting affirmation's antipode.

That's what the man wants to be able to say every day.

The rest is just the rest.

He orders an espresso, glass of water, and cannoli, waits for them and pops his statin before writing down the line that came to him strolling past Pasticceria Bruno on LaGuardia: *In the villa of Ormen stands a solitary candle.* It's the line that fits the melody he awoke from his red dreams humming: B, C, B, A minor.

Except why a solitary candle?

He doesn't know.

What does *Ormen* mean?

He hasn't a clue.

Or, wait, he does: that's the name of that tiny Norwegian village he visited decades ago. Yes: the country Hermione, that girl with the mousy hair, his magnificent first love, left him for in 1969 to romance someone else for a little while and appear in the film *Song of Norway*, that god-awful bore of a musical, about Edvard Grieg's early struggles, busy trying to cash in on *The Sound of Music*'s success.

Hermione and he were habit-forming.

Within minutes of meeting on the set of a BBC play in which they were both performing, they became romance junkies. Within two weeks they moved in together and became whatever it is that makes people feel uncannily connected and then searingly lonely, ruined, when they aren't with each other anymore.

For a year they shared the top floor of a three-story Victorian in South Kensington before he was anyone, she nineteen, he twenty-one and looking ten. It was him hearing himself demanding meals on the table just like his dad did, shirts ironed, a total affection, an unconditional attention, which he wasn't capable of returning himself, and Hermione had other lives she wanted to live, and it was the woman you love hopelessly announcing one evening she doesn't love you anymore, even though you both know she's lying, trying to talk herself into it even as she knows she can't, that she's saying those words because you each get only one existence, and she wanted hers to herself.

He lost touch with her immediately, completely, then met his little darling blowtorch and decided to become someone else.

Hermione's leaving crushed him, crushes him still. There was a fierce concentration to what they had, a continuous sense of newness and possibility that she pushed him out of when he wasn't expecting it.

Who thought forgetting wouldn't work?

Now the hours are reading, painting, writing, going for morning walks, doing business with Europe, phoning about the upcoming exhibition, the musical he has wanted to write ever since he was a kid, the new album climbing into the open before him, working out with a boxing coach, slipping into the Angelika to catch a new movie (and without paying twice, slipping into a second one), almost never venturing north of 14th Street, and being with his wife, simply *being* with her, calling Duncan, who watched his dad grow up in the seventies rather than the other way around, calling Lexi, who even at fourteen still delights in him taking her to MoMA and nattering about art as they wander from gallery to gallery—just to check in on them because he can, because this artlessness feels so good, because, precipitously, your family and friends have come to constitute both the living and the contrary.

Once it wasn't this luxurious sensation of time slowing, dilating, this space accruing in which you can be both hushed and rackety, the concerns of a career receding pleasantly, helplessly, behind you.

Now it is doing what you're doing without knowing what to call it anymore, taking pleasure in the fact that its name is too big to be caught in thought's failings.

That's the solitary candle.

Of course it is.

That's why he wore the navy-blue T-shirt with the film's title on it, *Song of Norway,* in Tony Oursler's video for "Where Are We Now?" He wanted to wave at Hermione from inside the time machine. In Berlin he heard she had moved to Papua New Guinea and married an anthropologist. In the late nineties he googled her one night and found what had happened to her, that she was even making some artwork of her own. That brought him a smile.

He meant the T-shirt to say: Hello, Hermione Farthingale. I hope you're doing okay. Look at us. We made it. I still think about you, you know. We're still living on and on in our year together. Just think of me and we're there.

It is B, C, B, A minor, the chords to the melody in his head, Hermione that ever-approaching fourth one.

This is what he prizes about cafés, it occurs to him, taking first a sip of espresso, reaching over and clipping off a corner of cannoli with his fork. He savors the sweet ricotta, the ability to enjoy it after leaving cigarettes behind and regaining his taste. Cafés allow things to come together. There's something distinctive in their din, the cozy congestion, the sparky scent of coffee, a peaceful corner amid commotion.

A way to cooperate with yourself, playing and listening at the same time.

In the thick of that thought he has another, coaxes his cell phone from his jeans pocket and calls his assistant Coco.

She answers on the second ring.

Boss?

Two things. Davy Jones would like to escort Mrs. Abdul-majid to the Village Vanguard this evening. A couple unobtrusive seats up on the what do you call it.

That gallery on the side? I'm on it . . . and?

And I have this I don't know what it is on my jaw I'd like to get looked at. Would you set me up with the dermatologist?

Done, she says. Where are you?

Beneath a faux Caravaggio in a Norwegian village on the southeastern border with Sweden in 1969. Why?

Go write, David Bowie. And if you can't be brilliant today, settle for being astounding.


## NEW ANGELS OF PROMISE

Home, passing the last few minutes before Iman's return, he is stretched out on the cream-colored leather couch, snicking through channels on the seventy-five-inch screen mounted on the far wall, the hallucinogenic radiance so acute, so extravagant, it seems to be spilling out from the center of his own cerebral cortex, while this guy with blond buzz cut believes loudly that his suburban ex-wife and her new husband molested his kids as the couple scream denials across the stage and Dr. Phil looks on smug yet somehow gratified ready to call a commercial break when maximum furor has been attained and Ukraine's army is launching military operations against separatists in Sloviansk helicopters skirting tree tops locals hunkered behind burning-tire barricades and *Family*

*Feud*'s Steve Harvey is asking *if you overheard the word MOOSE in a conversation what might they be talking about* and a somber Japanese official is declaring *the spread of polio is* and *get the total gym experience!* and Wolf Blitzer in his everything-is-end-lessly-911 expression is reporting *dramatic scenes from Southern California right now let's get back to the breaking news flames out of control a wildfire destroying houses* and Alexis Texas is getting doggied by Batman in the VIP lounge in back of some eighties nightclub yipping *yeah oh yeah give it to me baby!* in pipsqueak little-girl exclamations and *they killed Kenny!* and Anthony Doerr is *set phasers to* and Anthony Doerr is chatting animatedly about his new World War II novel *All the Light We Cannot See* opining *what you're forgetting is that this is a beautiful miracle you're talking to somebody very far away and all around us this electromagnetic radiation is carrying messages* and Miranda on *Sex in the City* is wondering aloud *what's the big mystery it's my clitoris not the Sphinx* and Boko Haram is taking credit for abducting eight more Nigerian girls and *Fast and Furious 6*'s Tej Parker is whining into his phone in the wake of this gargantuan-beetle super-tank erupting out the back of an armored eighteen-wheeler plunging down some remote desert highway *uh guys we gotta come up with another plan* and an achingly cute clan of meerkats is clustering on an outcropping like a brood of little old men wringing their hands in front of a synagogue on Shabbat and Barney Fife *heeeeere's . . . Johnny!* and Barney Fife *one of these days Alice* and Barney Fife is spouting in that goofy voice of his *if there's anything that upsets me it's having people say I'm sensitive* and the laugh track flares and Steve Tyler in a tight-fitting pink-sequined dress and spectacular high-set breasts is singing *dude looks like a lady* and a fighter pilot in black-and-white is *come on down* is *look up in the sky* is *this tape will self-destruct* is *a bird it's* is *Jane you ignorant nanu-nanu Lucy you got some splaining to do* a fighter pilot in black-and-white is adjusting his oxygen mask in the cockpit and three cartoon horses from some forties animation are whinny-laughing into the camera and a bus full of defeated rebels is withdrawing from Homs and the *isn't that book em Danno eat my special resistance* is *d'oh resistance* is *d'oh resistance* and the *isn't that special* and the machine guns *your final answer* are opening up on Bonnie and Clyde in that last scene of the look on *General Hospital* Olivia's face as she puts together the decisive pieces to realize Sonny has indeed slept with Barrack Obama is quipping in footage from the White House Correspondents' Association dinner *let's face it Fox you'll miss me when I'm gone cuz it will be harder to convince the American people that Hillary was born in Kenya* and Joe Cramer on *Mad Money* is shouting *they know nothing! they know* as Leonard Cohen gravels *everybody knows that the boat is leaking* and a preacher *like their father or their dog just died* a preacher is blaring face sweaty faith bulging *dial 1-900-GOD-SQAD that's 1-900-GOD-SQAD five dollars per call two dollars per minute seven minutes minimum you must be eighteen to lift that phone* and *everybody knows that you've been faithful give or take a night or two* and Conchita Wurst is schmaltzing *once I'm reborn you know I will rise like a phoenix* good god that song won the Eurovision contest last week didn't it only the front door is opening yes followed by that familiar suspension and then closing behind her and Iman is here he can feel her accumulation bathing the apartment as she moves through the rooms separating her from him and everything becomes simply a sunny late afternoon in New York City and everything becomes all right because everything becomes this.

## DIAMOND DOGS

### ANGIE BOWIE

Bowie's first wife: 1970 to 1980. Née Barnett. Manipulative, scheming, volatile, promiscuous, bitter, emotional nurse, mental housekeeper, creative ally, occasional redeemer, and perennial business adviser. American, she agrees to an open marriage with Bowie to secure her work permit in England. Mother of Zowie (from the Greek ζωή: *life*) Jones, born 1971, who became Joe, who became Duncan. Last contact with son: 1984. Long claims to have inspired The Rolling Stones' 1973 hit "Angie," an assertion Mick Jagger and Keith Richards consistently deny.

### BERLIN, 1976–1979

Shattered city surrounded by a dry mined moat. Seedy, poor, polluted, drab. A nexus where everyone thinks the next global inferno will mushroom any day and so keeps a packed suitcase beneath their bed just in case. In the west, military tanks and spectral black jeeps roll through the streets while Nazi war widows walk rat dogs through the overgrown parks. In the east, rubble from the Battle of Berlin is still heaped everywhere, the Soviets refusing to remove the monuments to German savagery. Yet also an energized, tireless, incredibly inexpensive hub of alternative culture brimming with bars, cabarets, drag reviews, discos, punk clubs, untamed galleries. Bowie: *The rest of Germany can't stand Berliners, and Berliners look down on the rest of Germany. That's why Hitler put his thumb on the city and decided to set up base here, because this was the most troublesome spot.* Bowie loves it. Bowie hates it. Bowie feels intoxicated. Bowie feels trapped. Bowie collects Nazi memorabilia, including Goebbels's old desk, which he displays in his apartment. He tells the story about how late one night, parked with Angie on the west side, sharing a cigarette, staring across a canal into the east, all at once there is a rap on the roof. A Red Army guard gestures for him to lower his window. Bowie does, and the guard asks for a light. You shouldn't be here, Bowie tells him. You should be over there. The guard spells out amiably he often traverses the secret tunnel running beneath the river to stretch his legs in this neighborhood. Like that.

MARC BOLAN

Lead singer: T. Rex. Glam rock pioneer. In 1977, career wobbly, fronts a six-part after-school series on ITV featuring both new and established bands. Final guest: David Bowie, with whom he performs "Heroes," at the end of which Bolan accidentally stumbles off the stage to Bowie's obvious glee as the credits roll. Days later the Mini that Bolan is in, soul-singer girlfriend Gloria Jones behind the wheel (Bolan never takes up driving because he fears automotive oblivion), skids out of control and rams a tree. He is killed instantly. Jones suffers a broken arm and jaw. Despite his relationship and baby (named Rolan Bolan) with Jones, Bolan is still legally married to June Child, a one-time gofer. The result is neither mother nor infant receives Bolan's inheritance. Bowie, Rolan's godfather, steps in to help out the couple financially until June Child dies of a heart attack while vacationing in Turkey seventeen years later, at which point Rolan acquires the estate.

## WILLIAM BURROUGHS

Bowie employs a version of Burroughs and Brion Gysin's cut-up method, whose randomness appeals to him, to generate some of his most startling lyrics: cf., most notably, *Diamond Dogs, Outside, Blackstar*. February 1974: *Rolling Stone* hires journalist Craig Copetas to drive Burroughs from his pared-down two-room flat in Piccadilly to say hello to Bowie in his elegant Chelsea townhouse and document what transpires between them. The joke, the reportorial tension, is that Burroughs doesn't know who Bowie is, save for the handful of lyrics Copetas has given him to read shortly in advance of the get-together. Both writer and rock star are clearly uncomfortable being thrown together, have almost nothing substantial to say to one another. The mutual interview meanders and unwinds. Burroughs: *You remember Ma Barker? Ma Barker doesn't like talk and she doesn't like talkers. She just sat there with her gun.*

## AVA CHERRY

Backing vocalist and Bowie's Black lover from 1972 to 1975, during his marriage to Angie. Travels the world with him. Hobnobs with celebrity heavyweights. Kind-hearted, compassionate, a-sparkle with love of and admiration for the superstar, who produces her proto-new wave album, *People from Bad Homes*, which, however, because of management issues, isn't released until 1995. Deep into cocaine derangements, Bowie determines his own management company has been spending most of his money behind his back on posh hotels, limos, and private jets from LA to Europe and back for his forty-plus entourage. He crumples emotionally, breaks up with Cherry, who has been trying on and off to mother him back to health and sanity, and pitches inward. Cherry in the rearview mirror: *I kept trying to find a way to not make it final.* Bowie, always the virtuoso at cutting, running scared and running away, makes sure it is just that.

## DON DELILLO

Fifty-three on Bowie's reading list: *White Noise* (1985). The fear of dying obsesses Babette, the narrator Jack Gladney's wife, to the point where she begins popping an experimental drug, Dylar, to repress her pulverizing sense of mortality. Jack, professor of Hitler Studies at a small midwestern college, gratified at cashing in on the intellectual goof called cultural studies, explains to one of his students that all plots move in one direction, deathward, something Bowie is achingly aware of most of his life, no more so than while making *Blackstar*, its title slang for the radial lesion on mammograms announcing breast cancer. During his final months, work becomes Bowie's Dylar. The album appears on Friday, January 8, 2016. Bowie becomes his own past two days later.

## TONY DEFRIES

Manager whom Bowie dubs his damager and sacks in 1975, wrecked by Defries's misappropriation of funds. Nevertheless,

DeFries deploys an ingenious strategy up front in Bowie's career: make it extremely difficult for anyone to get close to him. DeFries teaches the unseasoned singer how to act imperious: never open a door for himself; never pick up something dropped; never pass something at a restaurant; always stage aloofness; become enigmatic; amplify into something larger than himself. The strategy works in spades: Bowie plumes into rock'n'roll royalty, ascertaining in the process that acclaim and talent are unrelated concepts; that if you perform a character long enough, that character will eventually begin to perform you.

## T. S. ELIOT

The original cut-up king, atoms of whose "Love Song of J. Alfred Prufrock" (1915) and "Hollow Men" (1925) can be spotted in lyrics for "Eight Line Poem," and of whose *The Waste Land* (1922; sixteen on Bowie's reading list) in those for "Goodnight Ladies." Like Bowie, Eliot dabbles in the occult and criticizes democratic politics. Marries British woman, fragile Vivienne Haigh-Wood, even as Bowie marries American, feisty Angie. Recovering from a nervous breakdown in 1921, Eliot settles into a sanatorium in Lausanne, Switzerland, on the shores of Lac Léman, the area to which Bowie withdraws for much of the eighties and early nineties into a fourteen-room mansion built at the turn of the century by a Russian prince—until Iman complains that Switzerland is far too dull for her, prompting the couple in 1999 to shift their gravitational center to Manhattan.

## FANS

Distillate: on the 1974 Diamond Dogs tour in the US, where Bowie hasn't appeared live for more than a year, his rhapsodic fans expect him to turn up as Aladdin Sane (pun on Bowie's state of mind at the time: A Lad Insane). Instead, he steps onto the stage wearing slicked-back hair, baggy pleated pants, suspenders, and a white cotton shirt. During intermission, his devotees pour into the restrooms to wet down their own spiky hair, scrub the lightning bolts off their faces, and do what they can to modify the look of their ho-hum clothing that wasn't ho-hum an hour ago.

## BRIAN ENO

Keyboardist for Roxy Music, 1971–1973. Bowie's collaborator on the sonically revolutionary Berlin Trilogy—*Low* (1977), *Heroes* (1977), and *Lodger* (1979)—an amalgam of alternately anguished and euphoric funk, electronica, ambient soundscapes, cabaret, and guitar-based rock that, among other things, introduces millions around the world used to vanilla pop to what the Germans call *Neue Musik*. Eno plays synthesizer. Producer Tony Visconti uses an Eventide Harmonizer to alter the drums in a way, he is positive, he claims, *fucks with the fabric of time.* The outcome shapes many nineties musicians and bands, among them Radiohead, Björk, P.J. Harvey, Moby, and Blur. Bowie: *In some ways, those albums really captured a sense of yearning for a future that we all knew would never come. My complete being is within them. They are my DNA.* Eno and Bowie's last project together: *Outside* (1995), about which Eno wrote in his diaries: *I become a sculptor to David's tendency to paint. I keep trying to cut*

*things back, strip them to something tense and taut, while he keeps*
*throwing new colors on the canvas. It's a good duet. The only thing*
*missing was the nerve to be very simple.* The pair remains close for
nearly forty years. Separated geographically by the Atlantic,
they exchange regular emails between London and New York,
signing off with invented names: Mr. Showbiz, Milton Keynes,
the Duke of Ear. Eno describing their Berlin era: *It struck me as*
*paradoxical that two comparatively well-known people would be stag-*
*gering home at six in the morning, and he'd break a raw egg into his*
*mouth and that was his food for the day. We'd sit around the kitchen*
*table feeling a bit too tired—me with a bowl of crummy German cereal*
*and him with albumen running down his shirt.*

## HERMIONE FARTHINGALE

First love, 1968 to 1969. Bowie and she form a band, Feathers, that mixes music, poetry, and mime. Smitten, according
to friends at the time, he is ever the perfect gentleman. At dinner, he holds the chair for her, pushes it in, speaks in always
devoted inflections. And yet, according to others, he is also
domineering, demanding, wily, and incorrigibly promiscuous,
openly hopping from bed to bed without apology. Farthingale's solicitor dad disapproves vehemently of his daughter
moving in with a boy from Brixton who lacks prospects. He
believes Bowie is just using her and is relieved when she decides to put an end to her relationship with him so she can
pursue her own dance career on the set of *Song of Norway*. After
landing a further handful of stage and screen roles, she slides
into obscurity, marrying, settling, divorcing, docking at a yoga
studio in Bristol, Enya cycling on the sound system. In "Letter

to Hermione" from his eponymous 1969 album, Bowie puts into lyrics what he could never tell her to her face: *I'm not quite sure what I'm supposed to do, so I'll just write some love to you.* Unlike countless others caught up in his trajectory, decorous Farthingale maintains her silence through the decades about what they had. Their split marks the launch of Bowie's heavy cocaine use and ever-more-prodigal sex addiction.

## ROMY HAAG

Born Edouard Frans Verbaarsschott. Dutch dancer, singer, actress, former nightclub manager, and, throughout the seventies, one of the most famous transgender personalities in Europe. Claims she is the reason for Bowie's move to Berlin in 1976: *We saw each other at one of his concerts and that was it. Naturally I fell in love with his eyes. We knew we had to do some time together.* While married to Angie, Bowie lives on and off with Haag, while living on and off with Cherry, while living briefly with Kinder, trying to fathom what family might become once one frees oneself from the solely biological shackles. Haag's influence on his work is evident in his "Boys Keep Swinging" video, where Bowie appears in triplicate as a chorus of drag queens. Haag leaves home at thirteen to become a clown, then trapeze artist, and in due course a drag queen in Paris, where she commences living as a woman. In 1974 she opens Germany's most popular nightclub, Chez Romy Haag, with celebrity regulars Bryan Ferry, Bette Midler, Tina Turner, Freddie Mercury, Lou Reed, and occasional lover Mick Jagger. Haag: *David was such a boy back then. He was a little boy. A lovely little boy, who wanted to have some inspiration, who wanted to have some life. He always sat on the floor in the corner at the club (we didn't own any tables or chairs), just taking it all in.*

### DUNCAN ZOWIE HAYWOOD JONES

Film director, producer, writer, son. His birth in 1971 prompts Bowie to write the charming "Kooks" on *Hunky Dory*, whose opening lines read: *Will you stay in our lovers' story? If you do you won't be sorry.* Raised mostly by Scottish nanny in London, Berlin, Switzerland. Dreamed of becoming professional wrestler. Bowie granted custody after divorce from Angie in 1980. Jones marries photographer Rodene Ronquillo on November 6, 2012, the same day Ronquillo is diagnosed with breast cancer. Best-known movie: his first, *Moon*, the disturbing parable of another Major Tom lost in space, now on the far side of the moon at the conclusion of a solitary three-year stint mining helium-3, hallucinating, alone, forsaken as his identity shreds— just like Bowie's during the seventies when Jones witnessed his father fall short of maturing, repeatedly.

### LEXI JONES

Fifteen when her father dies. Throughout childhood, shielded from the media by Bowie and Iman. One of several blackboxes stacked along the interstate of his life.

### KATJA KINDER

Bowie and she help themselves to each other's bad dreams for three weeks in his umbral seven-room Schöneberg flat late in 1976, after Iggy Pop moves into his own digs across the courtyard. Aggressively Pollyanna-ish, below her tenacious involuntary smile Kinder is broken and forlorn at nineteen. A congenital planner, congenitally unmotivated and aimless, she conscientiously reformulates her experiential blueprint every three days as if this time she really means it. We cannot lay our hands on any more information about her. She seems to disperse into history sometime in 1977, although we do dig up a few fumy rumors circulating shortly thereafter that she relocates to Hamburg, where she winds up the sort of high school math teacher who keeps a flask of vodka in her purse, and/or relocates to Phoenix, Arizona, where she ends up the sort of massage therapist who keeps a dog-eared copy of *The Power of Now* on a shelf next to her healing crystals, scented votive candles, and repressed anguish. Given her disposition, these rumors seem as unlikely as likely to be based on fact.

## R. D. LAING

Eighty-six on Bowie's reading list: *The Divided Self: An Existential Study in Sanity* (1960), wherein the iconoclastic guru/mystic contrasts the experience of the ontologically secure individual with that of the one who *cannot take the realness, aliveness, autonomy and identity of himself and others for granted* and who consequently slips into ontological insecurity and psychosis often triggered by abnormal family relationships. Reading it, Bowie can't help thinking about his half brother, the emotional mutilation that defined his household as a child, his mother's detachment, the way his father bullied and excluded Terry from all things domestic, how icy that rail must have felt beneath Terry's cheek as the express train chaos-ed into the station.

DAVID MALLET

British director of such iconic music videos in the seventies and eighties as Queen's "Bicycle Race," Blondie's "Hanging on the Telephone," Boomtown Rats' "I Don't Like Mondays," and Bowie's "Boys Keep Swinging," "China Girl," and "Ashes to Ashes," the last at the time the most expensive ever made. It features scenes in stark noirish black-and-white set in a hospital-examination-room-cum-spaceship, in shadowy color set in a padded cell, and in psychotropic solarization on a beach. In it, Bowie wears a gaudy Pierrot costume, visual trademark of his Scary Monsters phase. A stock character from seventeenth-century commedia dell'arte, Pierrot is the epitome of the sad clown, the heartcracked fool pining for love, naïveté incarnate. The lyrics take us back once again to Major Tom floating out of control high, high above the earth, yet simultaneously huddled, frightened and unhinged, back on terra infirma, just like Terry at the asylum, just like part of Bowie himself, because everyone—even Davy Jones from Bromley, even Jareth the Goblin King from *Labyrinth*—now knows Major Tom is a junkie who has never done good things, never done bad, and the *shrieking of nothing is killing*. The expected future never arrives. The past is Marc Bolan's car always crashing, is wondering if she ever thinks of you, is the blood that starts to leak from your eyes one night because the cocaine has begun dissolving your sinuses. The video's tenor is somber, reflective, even mournful. Shot near Hastings, filming at one point is interrupted by an old man walking his Weimaraner. Mallet politely asks him if he would mind stepping out of the scene, gestures toward Bowie sitting next to the catering van, and asks: *Do you know who that is over there?* The old man responds: *Of course I do. It's some cunt in a clown suit.*

## GEORGE ORWELL

Twenty-eight on Bowie's reading list: *1984* (1949), whose first line reads: *It was a bright cold day in April, and the clocks were striking thirteen*, summoning the intense cold on the day of Bowie's birth, which causes the clock on Lambeth Town Hall, a five-minute walk from his house in Brixton, to strike, not twelve, but thirteen times. In 1973 Bowie decides to make a musical based on the novel. Sonia, the author's widow, refuses to grant rights, so Bowie makes the dystopian SF album *Diamond Dogs* instead, his original plans reverberating through such songs as "Big Brother," "1984," and "We Are the Dead"—the latter one of the last lines the protagonist Winston speaks to his first love, Julia, an instant before shock troops blast through the door, and drag them out to separate nightmares.

## TONY OURSLER

Longtime friend and American multimedia and installation artist whose repertoire of characters comprises neurotic, confused, abandoned teratoids in a continuous state of stupefied incredulity before the universe. Raised in Nyack, New York. Studied under Laurie Anderson at CalArts. One afternoon in the early nineties, Bowie simply shows up at his hovel of a studio at 175 Ludlow Street, a couple blocks east of Bowie's Lafayette Street penthouse, wanting to talk art. Oursler: *After his first heart attack, David went very quiet before reporting to me that he was reading approximately a book a day; he suggested I read one he loved that traced the fate of Oliver Cromwell's head, which had been cut off his disinterred body shortly after burial and traveled here and there. I am grateful to have had these kinds of discussions, and sometimes when he thought it had gotten too highbrow for me he would put a hand on my shoulder and say with a grin,* Tony, Tony, it's only rock 'n' roll. *Some have posited that the impulse to construct alternate identities is a model for another kind of consciousness, free from Freudian archetypes. Once, while visiting the Rubin Museum, David and I discussed Carl Jung's* Red Book *in relation to Jung's view of channeling characters while creating. That's a distinctly different view from Freud's, and, to my mind, Bowie's collection of personas offers just such a liberating trajectory, while also providing an alternative to the American cliché of rugged individualism and fixed, "authentic" identity.*

## IGGY POP

Bowie's accomplice, collaborator, and little brother by proxy. Born James Newell Osterberg Jr. on April 21, 1947, three months after Bowie. Raised in a trailer park in Ypsilanti, Michigan. Godfather of punk. Vocalist/lyricist for the Stooges, with whom he perfects the skills of stage diving, rolling on broken glass bare chested, self-cutting, and exposing himself to profoundly pleased audiences. Unable to control his heroin addiction, he checks himself into the UCLA Neuropsychiatric Institute in 1974. Bowie is one of his few visitors, showing up initially with a paper bag full of assorted drugs, which the staff makes him leave at the front desk. Bowie invites Pop to accompany him to Berlin so they can clean up together. He tours and makes four albums with Bowie: *Raw Power, The Idiot, Lust for Life*, and *Blah Blah Blah*. Describing their Schöneberg years,

Pop says: *The big event of the week was Thursday night. Anyone who was still alive and able to crawl to the sofa would watch* Starsky & Hutch. About Bowie's visit to Pop's parents' trailer: *The neighbors were so frightened of his car and the bodyguard they called the police. My father's a very wonderful man, and he said to David,* Thank you for what you're doing for my son. *I thought:* Shut up, Dad. You're making me look uncool.

## PROMISE, NEW ANGELS OF (1)

Artists acknowledging Bowie's influence: Arctic Monkeys, Boy George, Kate Bush, The Cure, Eurythmics, the Flaming Lips, Michael Jackson, Joy Division, the Killers (Brandon Flowers drops out of college to pursue music after hearing *Hunky Dory*), Lady Gaga, Lorde, Madonna, Marilyn Manson, Morrissey, Nine Inch Nails, Nirvana (Cobain's favorite: "The Man Who Sold the World"), Pet Shop Boys, Pixies, Prince, Sex Pistols, Siouxsie and the Banshees, the Smashing Pumpkins, the Smiths, U2. Zum Beispiel.

## PROMISE, NEW ANGELS OF (2)

The addictive personality. The search for the quick fix. The urge to risk everything, over and over again, which is to say sex with Charlie Chaplin's widow Oona (twenty-two years his senior), Marianne Faithfull, groupies (he estimates more than a thousand—among whom number girls as young as thirteen), his second manager Ralph Horton, Slash's mother Ola Hudson, dancer Melissa Hurley (twenty years his junior), Bianca Jagger, possibly Mick himself, mime Lindsay Kemp, record executive Calvin Mark Lee, Bette Midler, Susan Sarandon, Elizabeth

Taylor, Tina Turner, his assistant Tony Zanetta. *I think I was always a closet heterosexual,* Bowie telling a journalist, breaking into his characteristic angelic, self-effacing, impish smile.

### RAW

Art Spiegelman and wife Françoise's avant-garde comics anthology that ran from 1980 to 1986 and appears forty-seventh on Bowie's reading list. After an abysmal failure with *Arcade,* which goes under after only seven issues, Spiegelman swears he is finished with the form, but Françoise talks him into giving it a last go with a one-off compilation of such cartoonists as Chris Ware and Charles Burn. The first issue sells out almost immediately. The second features, among others, the first installment of Spiegelman's own *Maus,* which will reconceptualize the genre's power by telling his father's experiences in the Holocaust by casting the Nazis as cats, the Jews as mice, and the Poles as pigs.

### LOU REED

Guitarist, singer, principal songwriter for the Velvet Underground. Son of Toby and Sid Reed, an accountant who changes his name from Rabinowitz. Although Jewish, Reed maintains his real deity will always be rock'n'roll. Furious, competitive, resentful, stormy, conceited, inflexible, carnal, alcoholic, addicted, bullied at school, taken under wing by Delmore Schwartz at Syracuse University, frantically if sporadically into meditation as a mode of self-medication never as satisfying as drugs. When his parents find out about his fluid sexuality, they approach local psychiatrists in an attempt to unbisexual him. The psychiatrists prescribe several rounds of electroshock therapy. *The effect,* Reed reports, *is that you lose your memory and become a vegetable. You can't read a book because you get to page seventeen and have to go back to page one.* In college he adopts heroin, contracts hepatitis. When the Velvet Underground breaks up for good in 1970, he is forced at twenty-eight to live with Toby and Sid for a year, running office errands for his dad for forty dollars a week. Lives with a transgender woman named Rachel for half a decade. Meets his first wife, Bettye Kronstadt, in the midst of a three-day methamphetamine bender. He physically abuses her, leaving Bettye with facial bruises and blackened eyes on a regular basis. Friends characterize that relationship thus: *A marriage made in the emergency room.* His second wife: Sylvia Morales, art designer, manager, reading partner, maintains he is never anything but kind to her. Third wife: Laurie Anderson. Bowie coproduces Reed's solo album, *Transformer,* home to "Perfect Day," about his early love for Bettye, and "Walk on the Wild Side," about drag performers moving to New York to become prostitutes and/or denizens of Andy Warhol's Factory. Over dinner following a show at the Hammersmith Odeon in 1987, Reed asks Bowie to produce his next album. Bowie says he would be happy to— on the condition Reed sobers up. Reed leans across the table and punches Bowie in the face. Twenty-six years later, Reed dies of liver disease on a frisky Sunday morning in October at his home in East Hampton, taking in the trees outside his window while doing the famous twenty-one forms of tai chi, just his hands moving through the air, trying to disprove the assertion that there is no easy way out of this life.

## MICK RONSON

Ronno. The Keith Richards to David Bowie's Mick Jagger in the Spiders from Mars. Morrissey: *He was the balls to Bowie at that time. He was the engine.* Bowie: *He provided this strong, earthy, simply focused idea of what a song was all about. And I would flutter all around him on the edges and decorate. I was sort of the interior decorator.* Yorkshire working-class. Lapsed (very lapsed) Mormon. A man's man's man, that oddest of hormonal species, but never built to be a front man. Good friend all the way back to the days of the Hype. Trained in classical piano, recorder, violin, he supplied Bowie with string arrangements as well as lead guitar. Bowie and he last took the stage together on April 20, 1992 for the Freddie Mercury Tribute Concert to play "All the Young Dudes," which Bowie had written for Mott the Hoople. Died of liver cancer on April 29, 1993 at forty-six. Bowie said he was too distraught to play at Ronno's memorial concert. Trevor Bolder, fellow band member in the Spiders from Mars: *But when Freddie Mercury died, Bowie was straight on stage because it was in front of millions of people . . . . He wouldn't get there for Mick Ronson's because it wasn't a big enough audience.*

## CORINNE SCHWAB

Coco. Personal assistant with Jewish ancestry, perhaps closest friend, alleged intermittent lover, provoker of Angie's ire, lifeguard, guard dog, partition between Bowie and everything else (cf. *provoker of Angie's ire*), yet another nanny and surrogate mother (quite possibly the most significant), yet another blackbox, unceasingly discreet, nearly invisible, silent, nevertheless by his side for forty-six years. Friends commenting that

Bowie and she looked as if they had been married decades. Coco is the subject of "Never Let Me Down"—e.g., *When I believed in nothing I called her name.* Designated Lexi's guardian, should anything happen to Iman before their daughter turns eighteen. Bequeathed two million dollars in Bowie's will. (Two million? Given her devotion, the enormousness of his estate? Really?)

## TONY VISCONTI

American record producer, musician, singer. All said and done, you can count on the fingers of one hand all the people who really meant something to Bowie over the course of his career, and, if you're being honest, it is probable that that one hand holds several fingers too many. Visconti, however, would always be numbered among them. Works with, among others, the Dandy Warhols, Fall Out Boy, Gentle Giant, Paul McCartney and Wings, the Moody Blues, T. Rex, the Stone Roses. Leaves hometown of New York in 1967, transplanting to London, meets Bowie through Marc Bolan, hitting it off because of their shared musical loves: Frank Zappa's free-form improvisations and sound investigations; Velvet Underground's merger of the aurally innovative and pared-down rock-as-prophecy; the Fugs' lewd, comedic countercultural songs in the key of the middle finger. Bowie and Visconti form one of the great artist/ producer partnerships in music history, working on fourteen albums together, among which: the second, *David Bowie*; the Berlin Trilogy; the penultimate, *The Next Day*; and the last, *Blackstar*. Writing Bowie's afterword: *His death was not different from his life. It was a work of art.*

ANDY WARHOL

August 6, 1928: born Andrew Warhola in Pittsburgh to a coal-miner father and homemaker mother from Austria-Hungary. Artist, film director, producer, pop art nobility fixated on the nexus of advertising, celebrity culture, ironized sincerity, and what used to be thought of as Art with that capital A: *What's great about this country is that America started the tradition where the richest consumers buy essentially the same things as the poorest. You can be watching TV and see Coca-Cola, and you know that the President drinks Coca-Cola, Liz Taylor drinks Coca-Cola, and just think, you can drink Coca-Cola, too.* June 3, 1968: shot through both lungs, spleen, stomach, liver, and esophagus by Valerie Solanas, a separatist feminist advocating the elimination of all men from the planet. Warhol nearly succumbs, suffers physical repercussions for the rest of his life, requiring him to wear a surgical corset. Bowie recounting their first meeting, which transpires shortly after Warhol returns to the Factory after Solanas's assassination attempt: *So I stepped off the elevator and right into a camera lens. He took my photo before I could say anything and it struck me he doesn't look like flesh. Clearly he's reptilian. Yellow complexion. White wig. These little glasses. He's the wrong color to be a human being. I extended my hand and he pulled back. I tried to make small talk, but nothing happened. Then he saw my shoes. They were gold.* I adore those, *he said.* Where did you get them? *He wanted to be a cliché. He wanted to be available in Woolworth's. We tried to talk a little more, then I said I had to be going. I left knowing as little about him as a person as when I went in.*

# BLACKOUT

—scribbles Alec Nolens on his canary legal pad in blue ink, we scribble, the third day of his sabbatical having somehow adjusted into the forty-eighth of mine, most marked by a morning's pleasure in resisting linearity's limitations, the axiological and the genealogical, an afternoon's stroll through breezy, leafy Prenzlauer Berg to Anna Blume, my choice café, named after the subject, by the way, of a 1919 Kurt Schwitters poem, for my daily latte and slice of Apfelkuchen (sans whipped cream—one must know one's boundaries), perhaps a visit to a museum or gallery, trailed by an evening's reading and note-taking with occasional excursion to a movie in the Hackescher Höfe Kino or jazz across town at the cramped A-Trane.

With my writing it is always the same drill. Some days nothing can go wrong. Some days nothing can go right. Some days there are simply too many words in the English language. Some days there are not enough, syntax is a minefield, ideas are missing in action.

Some days an unexpected discovery dazzles out from the middle of a clause. Others a drizzly brain fog clings to slate thought-streets in some rotting medieval village of the mind.

Lather. Rinse. Repeat.

How odd to be back at it after all this time, after that first study an aeon ago (lush language the actual indecent love affair eventuating in Nabokov's special favorite, *Lolita* [1955])— number nine, it turns out, synchronicity never ending, on

Bowie's book list), which reeled in my tenure and promotion, the second (Charles Mingus's apparition wafting through contemporary literature and culture—n.b. listen to the fifth line in the last stanza of "Suffragette City" to hear Bowie wave at track three of *Oh Yeah,* "Wham Bam Thank You Ma'am"), which hatched my full professorship, the odd essay and review left askew along the road's shoulder . . . and continuous wonder at where they all came from, the startle that rounding this lap of life I might just have another book in me which I genuinely care about, free from yawny professional presumptions.

I can sense how stubbornly this one has rooted itself inside me, unwilling to get out of my head because—because there's that word again, causality's hocus-pocus burrowed deep into our conjunctions, when in the final analysis it's really all *and* and *except* down, down, down the paratactical rabbit hole.


I thought I was done. I hoped I was done. I was betting I was done. I set my writing aside in favor of the sea of perplexed faces in my classrooms and whatever the local cause of the week was, trying to sway myself into thinking I could accomplish more Out There than In Here, on paper, amid the brain's empathy, although I could never quite explain to friends what I meant.

In any case, as luck would have it, my psyche incubated other proposals behind my back. Incrementally, secondary sources began rising like a slow tide around me, photographs, books, newspaper columns, miscellaneous scraps, all in the form of an appeal, a proposition, a challenge to decode and think again and feel again with something like intensity again, and so here I am this morning, June's bird gibber constant in those courtyard trees beyond my cracked-open window, never sure if this thing before me is sailing or sinking, staring down one more blackbox: Bowie and Iman's relationship.

Where did *that* come from?

What was it like?

Iman and Bowie wouldn't say. Try hazarding a guess, and all you do is bump your nose against the glass pane of that pact they kept between themselves for nearly a quarter of a century: do what you need to do to further your personas and portfolios, only at the end of each day David Bowie and Iman must remain propped against the wall in the hallway, two cardboard cutouts, while the other pair reanimate themselves on the far side of the door—which means, exactly, what?

Beats me.


You seem to know things, which is to say you have ferreted out a few thousand facts, more or less. You can tell people, for instance, that *Iman* means *faith* in Arabic, that she was born July 25, 1955 in Mogadishu, Somalia, to a gynecologist mother and diplomat father—though early in her career she deliberately aided and abetted the hoax that she had been unearthed herding cattle in the African bush to spike the exotic stock of her tall stature, slender figure, long neck, full lips, mysterious accent, and lustrous cinnamon skin.

From age four, you can say, she attended a Catholic boarding school in Egypt, and, when Somalian politics blighted, the family fled to Kenya, where Iman briefly studied political science at the University of Nairobi before marrying a Hilton executive at eighteen. That marriage dematerialized when she moved to the US to pursue modeling, famed photographer Peter Beard having stumbled across her on a street in the Kenyan capital. In 1977 she crept charily into a second marriage with LA Lakers forward Spencer Haywood, whose ho-hum performances on the court earned him the nickname Spencer Deadwood among sports writers, and whom she ditched nine years later, promising herself never to speculate on a third lockup.

A not undevout Muslim who labels herself a lapsed feminist (cf.: *The struggle is real, but so is God.*), you can say, Iman is impressively fluent in Somali, Arabic, Italian, French and English. She functions as cosmopolitan plexus where ethnicity, religion, politics, pop culture, and the game of glitz coalesce into an uneasy confederacy, which includes breast inflation to a 34B (*I was raised to treat my body as a temple, but I thought there was something wrong with the temple.*), getting married to Bowie in an Episcopal church rather than a mosque, vowing publicly to cook dinner for her hubby every evening, making nice through her philanthropy, and making gobs of money through her Global Chic clothing line (featuring anything except real fashion; neither global nor chic) on the Home Shopping Network, and Iman Cosmetics (featuring makeup for women of color) everywhere.

Her autobiography, *I Am Iman*, isn't an autobiography.

It sheds zippo light on the private.

So we must look elsewhere for refracted glimpses of her connection with Bowie and Bowie's with her. She tried him on, she disclosed, and found a soulmate fit, but: *I fell in love with David Jones. I did not fall in love with David Bowie. Bowie is just a singer, an entertainer. David Jones is the man I met.*

When she interviewed him for *Bust Magazine* in the fall of 2000, a decade after they first met at a dinner party (Bowie: *I did something really corny the next day. I invited Iman to afternoon tea*—despite the fact that he hated tea and ended up drinking coffee instead), eight years after they were wed (Bowie: *You would think that a rock star being married to a supermodel would be one of the greatest things in the world–it is*), for which he got his gnarly canary smoker's teeth replaced with a shiny white straight set of crowns, taming his rebel mouth—when Iman interviewed him for *Bust Magazine*, she posed this as her last question: *What do you think makes relationships between men and women work?*

Bowie answers, deadpan: *Complete and absolute generosity with the duvet.*

It's blackbox blackout beneath blackbox blackout.
    Who cares?
    Nobody.

Come on: Who cares?
    Everybody.
    Really?
    At least a little, right?
    Otherwise, why are we reading on?

As I say, my interest in Bowie accrues at the inverse of his youth. When we're in our teens, our twenties, we believe effortlessly that we choose *cha-cha-cha-changes*. At some point it becomes increasingly clear that change is also choosing us. Somewhere in our late forties, early fifties, we turn into a batch of letters somebody sent a long time ago. We are no longer on the way. We have arrived, wherever we are, for better, for worse, for both, till death do us part.

The harrowingly fundamental question remains: Who do you become when you become yourself?

Yourselves?

That's the big ask that bobs up after all the peewee ones.

And the clear, conclusive answer is: Nobody knows.

If challenging texts—think *Ulysses*; think *Tender Buttons;* think *Gravity's Rainbow*—teach us how to read them (and they do with a vengeance), what results when we encounter one like Bowie&Iman, a text that makes it its business to italicize its own illegibility?

What results when unreadability *is* the interpretation?


That didn't go well. Let me try again. Julian Barnes's glistening critifiction *Flaubert's Parrot* (1984) appears forty-third on Bowie's reading list. Geoffrey Braithwaite, the novel's narrator, its beautifully rigorous reader, an academically disposed retired doctor obsessed with all things Flaubert, especially (I have no idea why) *A Sentimental Education* (1869) and (so much so) *Madame Bovary* (1856), has thrown himself, in the wake of losing Ellen, his wife, first to adultery and then to suicide, into the minutiae of Flaubertiana in order to stuff the searing nothing not-ing at his core.

*By immersing himself in the personality of others*, Flaubert knows, *he forgot his own, which is perhaps the only way not to suffer from it.*

Amen.

Braithwaite gets that, and hence knows his undertaking is an always-already lost cause and because.

He knows something else, as well: that getting a historical person—which is to say any person—right is wrong.

It can't be done.

There is no such thing as an accurate account of somebody's existence, although there can certainly be and ever are vastly inaccurate ones. That's the sham that keeps biographers and memoirists in bankable business.

The symbolic flag for this realization in Barnes's novel is Lulu, the stuffed parrot Gustav kept on his desk while composing "A Simple Heart," and which Braithwaite stumbles across in Rouen's Musée Flaubert. The difficulty comes when, not long after that initial encounter, Braithwaite stumbles across a second stuffed parrot alleged to be Lulu, this one at the Croisset pavilion where Gustav lived the last thirty-seven years of his life riddled with various venereal diseases and barreling toward the brick wall of a cerebral hemorrhage at fifty-eight. Both docents—the fellow at the museum, the fellow at the pavilion—claim with comprehensive French hauteur that his parrot is the real taxidermied deal.


Another way of putting this: history is a mode, not merely of dates and data, but also of writing moves and belief, which is to say a mode of reading, which is to say a series of blindnesses, which is to say a conglomeration of misgivings, misconceptions, and misinterpretations.

We can't go back, no matter what.

As much as physicists and New Age claptrappers would like to pretend otherwise, time's arrow is stuck on fast-forward.

(Sorry about that.)

This knowledge, if we let it penetrate us even for a second, shatters our wits almost as quickly as it does our hopes.

We never find history waiting for us like an Uber at the airport. We make it up as we go along. Not from whole cloth, certainly, but from jigsawed, biased bits.

We decide which dates and data to foreground, which to background, which to drop, which to jump up and down about, which to sweep discreetly under the manuscript. Then we arrange what's left into a certain order that, as Hayden White reminds us in *Metahistory: The Historical Imagination in the Nineteenth Century* (1973), necessarily turns history into a beeline narrative, which in other contexts we would recognize as generic romance, satire, comedy, or tragedy, depending— never, however, into the disheveled thing itself.

How could it be otherwise?

History thereby regularly applies that catty conjunction used by doctors, geologists, mathematicians, and literary wannabes alike in order to appear to explain (and hence explain away) what occurred, when, why, how, and to whom.

In *A Poetics of Postmodernism* (1988), Linda Hutcheon tunes into White's wavelength and converts what she hears there into her own station: *historiographic metafiction*—i.e., fictions about history that understand that they are *fictions* about "history," which can never accurately manifest history, but rather only the problematization of the very idea of pastness.

*Tony, Tony, it's only rock 'n' roll.*


Iman and Bowie maintain they are wholly uninterested in persona's pretense.

Rather, for them, they say, it's the something supposedly far more authentic deep down inside that they care about.

The former carefully fabricates her yarn to make sure it is the one she wants the world to recall about her, even as the latter becomes Geoffrey Braithwaite personified, obsessive writer and reader of superstar David Bowie, archivist and curator of Davy Jones's avatar, amasser of a vast collection of articles relating to said avatar's career, among which resides a tissue blotted with his lipstick, the celebrity counterpart of some saint's finger or femur stuck in a gold-leafed jug, pop culture's nuzzle into faith and exaltation.

People pay twenty bucks on weekdays and twenty-five on weekends to hop through the looking glass into the cathedral whose name is *David Bowie is . . .* , a recasting of museum space into holy sheen, theatrical spectacle, sacred awe, and the promise of redemption through a surge of film montages, soundtracks, and three hundred objects (working notes, sketches, lyrics, artworks, videos, costumes, even an old coke spoon) from his seventy-five-thousand-object personal collection—all assiduously laid out to make the visitor feel a Protestant's divine intimacy with the theorem in question's creative practices, processes, and products, at the end of which awaits the blessed gift shop where you, too, can buy your way into heaven.

(Coca-Cola, anyone?)

At the entrance, we are confronted by an illustrative choice: which of two doorways to step through. They are of equal size, indicating both equal validity and no central path into the textual labyrinth toward our narrativization of D.B.

*Walking through the rooms,* one reviewer wrote, *is like walking through parts of his brain.*

But it isn't.

It isn't at all.

That's missing the point entirely.

Walking through the rooms (in 2014, in Kreuzberg at the Martin-Gropius-Bau, after my early afternoon Apfelkuchen and latte—sans whipped cream) is like walking through a carefully constructed hallowed funhouse of feints, surfaces, and irredeemable promises.

That feeling of relishing *David Bowie is . . .* is precisely the feeling of relishing who David Bowie isn't.

The exhibition's meaning lies squarely in its title's ellipsis of uncertainty.


## LOOKING FOR SATELLITES

Huh, says the dermatologist, unable to understand what he is looking at.

Umbral scruff at eleven a.m., a certain suburban New Jersey neglect for hairstyle, Dr. Ancell Soen, belly parting lab coat, leans into his dermatoscope, squinting.

Gently palpates the anomaly.

Scrapes it with the edge of one glass slide until a cell flurry has sprinkled onto another held beneath it.

He excuses himself to search for fungal spores under his microscope down the hall.

From her seat across the examination room, Coco, shortish reddish hair, makeup-less, understated pearl earrings dangling, tries to distract the patient with her thoughts concerning the new Robert Heinecken retrospective at MoMA, the one she took in yesterday during her free time: his eerie gray-and-white paraphotographs created by appropriating and re-processing images from magazines, product packaging, and television.

A cross assembled from shots of creepy antique dolls.

Negative of a sexy model in sunglasses and bra from a fashion magazine where the images on the next page have bled through, vexing what the viewer sees, foreground and background fused and confused, body and arrangement. At the top, the phrase *ARE YOU REA* without any concluding punctuation, which could mean *Are you a person named Rea?*, or perhaps *Are you ready?*, *Are you real?*, *Are you readable?*, or something else completely.

You'd like it, Coco says.

Is that my view? the patient asks.

Outside the examination room an old-time phone or smartphone made to sound like an old-time phone rings twice, quits. Coco and the man wait to see if it will ring again.

When it doesn't, Coco continues: Don't you know I know what you think before you think it? Heinecken decided media is so ubiquitous we should talk about it as the only nature we ever actually experience anymore.

Did you see the dandruff?

What?

On his left collar?

Whose collar, Davy?

He shouldn't be wearing indigo shirts. Not at this stage of his life. He's in his, what, early-graying midforties, and totally in the dark on the matter. You would assume he has someone to tell him this, wouldn't you.

But, yes, I think you'd like it.

How we feel ourselves growing older every second in planes and airports, watching YouTube, scrolling through Facebook. That's why they really exist: to make us sense the years we're missing. What did he say it looked like again?

Who?

The doctor. The thing.

The letter *e*. He said it looked like a nearly microscopic letter *e*.

And you don't find that disconcerting?


A rap at the door and Dr. Soen hustles back in, announcing: I got nothing. No spores, no fungus. No fungus, I'm guessing biopsy. I'm guessing send it over to the lab for assessment to be on the safe side. Only I should tell you you'll have a scar.

A scar, repeats the man.

A tiny scar. Yes.

How tiny? asks Coco.

Tiny like a permanent shaving nick.

But I don't think I want a tiny permanent shaving nick, the man says.

Just to be on the safe side, says the dermatologist. You know. It's probably et cetera. But I'd recommend it.

Dr. Soen steps over to the sink, uses his elbows to manipulate the long silver faucet levers. Scrubbing with a sudsy yellow-orange soap, he asks over his shoulder: Did John Lennon really once tell you glam rock was just rock'n'roll with lipstick on?

He did.

Why do I love that so much?

No one will even notice, Coco says. It will be too small to notice, almost.

*Zugzwang*, says the man after terse contemplation.

The dermatologist: *Zugzwang?*

German for that moment in chess, you know, where a player has to move, except any move will make his position worse than it was before he made the move, except he has to move anyway, because those are the rules.

Those Germans, says Dr. Soen, laying out a biopsy kit on the aluminum counter by the sink as if dealing cards. What kidders.

## EIGHT-LINE POEM

Three weeks later, angling in front of the bathroom mirror the better to trim his sideburns, he remarks the anomaly's return, this man suddenly in his late sixties, this man who looks fifteen years younger than he is.

He considers what the event signifies, the magnitude of today never remaining yesterday.

How there is this line of poetry he can't quite place—he is fairly sure, regardless, it is poetry—that woke him this morning: *Nothing is quite so beautiful as the trains I've missed.* It hung there in the middle of him, luminous, as he breached into consciousness.

Wandering through the living room, atmosphere made hot by the augmenting late-spring sun, he focuses on inhaling through his nose, exhaling through his pursed lips, just that.

The breath in.

The breath out.

He stalls at the waist-high cactus in front of one of the windows and, counting air conditioners protruding like half a dozen dirty white punctuation marks from the six-story brick building across Lafayette, phones Coco, who phones the dermatologist's office, whose secretary assures her they can fit him in at the end of the day, then he walks into the panic room off the bedroom, swings shut the heavy metal door, bolts it, and assumes the lotus position on the mattress in the corner among the various pitches the absence of sound makes.

Back in the examination room, listening to the dermatologist speaking as if from inside a closet, the man is sharply aware how with each second the world here becomes a tiny bit more real, its edges a tiny bit more spiky, himself occupying one of those occurrences that, even as he is living it, he knows he won't ever get to leave behind.

—which isn't unusual, Dr. Soen is saying when the man rejoins the conversation, because it seemed like we got everything. The results came back negative. Only it appears there was some what do you want to call it, some surplus we missed, which is it happens.

Some surplus, the man repeats.

It gets our attention when it grows back so fast. Not to et cetera. Just we go in a little deeper this time, cut out a little bit more, make a wider margin of safety.

A wider margin of safety, the man says.

Only I should let you know: the scar? It will become slightly more generous. But, well, life.

Half-listening to Coco asking follow up questions, the dermatologist answering, the man gains an acute sense of recollections accumulating inside him, a school of memory remoras clinging to the flanks of his reflections.

They have nothing to do with this room.

Three or four at first.

Out of nowhere, twenty, thirty teeming in.

Somewhere out there the dermatologist injects a numbing agent around the anomaly.

One minute, two, and from somewhere else there comes the blunt pressure of a preliminary incision, although what strikes the man is, vivid as those recollections are—he can see scenes in glittery detail; remember the memory of touches; the memory of smells—he won't ever be able to weave his way back into the moments themselves.

It's the strangest thing, inhabiting the past while grasping how unconditionally he is barred from it.

Always there.

Always not.

Always both and neither.

It is the man thinking: *All of us are learning to get old for the first time.*

It is the man thinking: *None of us will get to do it again.*

## WARSZAWA

The scalpel's pressure irises into a Berlin punk club in 1976.

Cigarette smoke. Beer-and-vomit stink.

Some shirtless, sweaty, skeletal guy on stage attacks his guitar with a dull saw, a lunatic wake marking the fifteenth anniversary of the Wall's construction.

Ringing it all—the place only seventy, seventy-five feet in circumference—a miniature replica of the fortified concrete-and-wire barrier made out of cake with ash-colored icing.

At the stroke of midnight, the guy on stage drops his guitar into a flood of feedback, raises his arms in some sort of victory salute, and bays at the ceiling, at which sign the club's occupants leap upon the cake, hammering it with their fists, tearing at it with their teeth, smashing it into ashen mush that they shove into their faces, rub into their spiked hair, lob at others around them like sloppy snowballs.

That isn't what the man finds so affecting.

What the man finds so affecting is how, afterward, everybody just stands around, cake smeared across their mouths, chunks clumped on the sides of their heads, leather jackets, black T-shirts, sliding down their jeans, arms dangling at their sides, each suspended by him or herself in the near darkness of their private isolation tank.


And yet it is also 1971, three months before the Electric Circus closes in the East Village, and tonight the Velvet Underground is up, a band the man has never seen live before, only heard on vinyl.

He arrives early, eases to the lip of the stage to make sure Lou Reed, whose music he tumbled into as a teen back in Bromley, can see him sing along to all the lyrics.

He aims to become the outward quintessence of zealous fan.

After the show, the man makes his way to the side of the stage, near the dressing room door, hangs back while others pay tribute. He hates meeting new people he admires. It always seems as if he's shaking hands with apparitions. Nonetheless, he collects his nerve, and, when the crowd scatters, steps forward and knocks. The drummer answers. The man effuses. The drummer smirks. The man asks if he might have a couple minutes with Lou. The drummer tells him to wait there. The dressing room door shuts.

Not long and it is Lou Reed not smiling at him, the two of them sitting side by side on the stage edge talking about song-writing for ten minutes, at which point Lou, clearly growing bored, says he has to get going, and the man overdoes the thank-yous and exits onto St. Mark's Place, unimaginably content.

Next day, he recounts his meeting to Iggy Pop with pride skimming through his voice.

Iggy studies him, an eyebrow centimeters up, and he barges into laughter.

Davy, man, he says, Davy—Lou left the band last August. You must have been talking to his replacement, Doug Yule. That's fucking *priceless*. Tell me about it all one more time, will you? *Please.*


And it is 1977, Katja rolling over to face him in bed among all the hungover afternoon shadows, nose pink from crying, bobbed black hair a mess from not leaving this stale nest for three days, breath a disappointment of fetid gin martinis and Gitanes, chili-pepper-red lipstick smudged from sex, releasing a memo from the other side of joy: I've been thinking, Davy. I've been thinking maybe I'm too lazy to invest in a meaning-ful relationship.

She curls into the crook of his shoulder, tucks her legs beneath his.

I'm not an altogether bad person, she adds, am I?

It is the man, now thirty, still blurry and buzzed from last night, the floor at some point having flown up and hit him, ab-sorbing the incoming information, and, aspiring to locate the crown molding through gloom, saying a minute later: Don't forget self-indulgent, Liebling. You're self-indulgent, too. If it's not all about you, it's all about nothing.

You believe that?

You love to talk about loving people, so long as it's at a distance. Universal love is easy for you because it's about the separation you can keep from others.

Fuck you, David Bowie. Sometimes you can be a scary monster. Leave me alone.

No, no—it's okay. Don't be mad. I'm just like you. That's why I get it. We never look at each other when we look at each other. We spend all our time together looking into mirrors.

Katja mulls this over until she seems to fall asleep snuggled against him.

When the man is sure the conversation is behind them, she whispers against his neck: Are we nihilists?

You're going to find it rather difficult to catch us in a category.

. . .

. . .

. . .

You're saying what, Katja says. You're saying all we can do is live in this now we have. You're saying all we can do is not ask questions and enjoy ourselves. That's what you're saying.

I'm saying Eastern gibberish is remarkably last week, Liebling. Mahayana, Theravada, faux herbal remedies, Gaea, karma, chakras—excuse me while I nod off for a second . . . there we go . . . that's better—the mass hallucinations known as astrology and reincarnation, getting grounded, letting go, staying centered . . .

. . .

. . .

. . .

Unicorns, he appends. Don't forget the unicorns. Santa Claus, Easter bunnies, other assorted Bullshit Speak. I think maybe it's time to take off our stupid, soothing as it surely is.

. . .

. . .

. . .

. . .

. . .

And now there is simply this couple lying quiet and atangle in a shadowy, musty seven-room flat in Schöneberg, considering what has just passed between them, what it implies and what it doesn't, how there always seems to be another part of love to kill.

Slowly they notice themselves concentrating on each other's skin until it is impossible to tell where one of them stops and the other commences, and there is Katja's voice whispering into his neck again, asking: Why are we like this, Davy?

Have you heard of D. T. Suzuki?

Let's *bumsen machen.*

Daisetsu Teitaro Suzuki. Japanese scholar of Buddhism.

Make us a drink and let's *bumsen machen*, Davy. *Das wird uns helfen zu forget.*

One of his books ends with a poem by a monk describing his attainment of enlightenment.

Okay.

You know what the poem's last line says?

It says let's be sleepy in our little hologram world while listening to good Krautrock.

It says: *Now that I'm enlightened, I'm just as miserable as ever.* You know what that means?

*Keine Ahnung.*

It means this is a hell of a lot of work to go through to reach where we've been all along, don't you think?


It's 1977, yet also 2014, not now, a week later, Dr. Soen explaining the results of the biopsy are inconclusive, he wants to run a couple more tests, which, over the course of the next month, will become more and other tests, yet it is also still 1973 and Truman Capote is proclaiming to the man in the midst of some noisy party, pressed so close he can actually register Capote's saliva mites spattering his face, *let's be clear about one thing, sweetie—Mick Jagger is about as sexy as a pissing frog,* and also still 1961, Terry's hand reaching toward him with his copy of *On the Road,* redheaded model in low-cut top and chartreuse pants monopolizing the cover, and 1994, the man strolling hand in hand with Iman after dinner along the boardwalk of Lac Léman, commenting *just imagine, love: nobody in the whole world is thinking about us this very second . . . isn't it phenomenal?,* 1994 and still 2014, the patient unexpectedly standing in a beflowered hospital gown next to the giant white cylinder of an MRI machine, ass chilly, prick shriveled, explaining to the technician in Mylanta-green scrubs and wilted gray pompadour that he is claustrophobic, seriously so, which leads to a phone call, which leads to a longish wait, which leads to another phone call, and next an IV has been inserted into

the man's arm and *wow, wow, wow,* he is flying through interstellar space inside a cramped capsule, cosmic rays dancing
through him, radio waves of illumination, a sledgehammer
banging on the nickel-steel alloy encasing him, ground control
long out of reach, it creeping up on him he might have got the
recollection completely wrong, yes, that thing with the Ber-
lin-Wall cake befell Iggy, not him, come to think of it, it was
Iggy who recounted it to the man, not the other way around,
wasn't it, or maybe he got it right after all, it really did happen
to him, he can't—and all of a sudden that growing mnemonic
dissonance in his chest dissolves into a Zen aphorism he may
or may not have just made up—he can't tell anymore—he can't
tell anything anymore—his spaceship spinning violently end
over end through stardust and void—*if something is boring after
two minutes, try it for four, and if it is boring after four, try it for eight,
sixteen, thirty-two, because eventually you will figure out that, if you
spend enough time with anything, it is impossible for it to become other
than spellbinding.*

It is deep space then and two seconds ago, two weeks, ninety minutes from now, thirty-four years since he first takes the
stage at the Booth Theater on West 45th to play Joseph Merrick, the Elephant Man, carrying Merrick's macrocephaly, in-
discriminate bone growth, wildfire tissue masses inside him,
opening his mouth to say in the clotted accent he developed
for the role *sometimes I think my head is so big because it is so full
of dreams,* even as Dr. Soen leans forward in the chair across
from Coco and him, hands on knees, delivering his evalua-
tion, saying—and it is 1994, Iman complaining as they sit side

by side before the fire in their mansion, sipping Riesling, that their life in Switzerland is far too sluggish for her tastes, *I love the energy of New York* she telling him, and the man responding *then you should stick your finger into an electric socket,* 1994 and 1961, the Berlin Wall growing in black-and-white on the TV downstairs and Terry rapping on his door for decades in order to bestow upon him his very own copy of *On the Road,* booning him with a benediction he will never let go of—*I think this might open a window or two for you, Davy, it did for me*—and that evening coming across lines like *what is that feeling when you're driving away from people and they recede on the plain till you see their specks dispersing?–it's the too-huge world vaulting us, and it's good-bye*—because that is the book through whose words reading becomes living, force and friction, the volume of another soul pressing against you on the other side of every sentence, so much better than meeting people face to face because it means you're meeting their best and worst selves at once, and in 1973 Duncan is taking his first wobbly steps in a dressing room before a concert in Paris, nanny holding his arms up over his head for support, this little grinning chimp, even as in 1986 the man hears himself tell a journalist, although he tries to stop himself from saying it aloud, ashamed at his own swift meanness, that Angie has as much insight into the human condition as a walnut, and now those words are in the universe forever, he can't take them back, what was he thinking, but by 1998 he is unable to summon up much at all about his ex-wife anymore, how did that—not their ten years together, not the buffoonery of their bond, those fights, their mutual manipulation and malice, their protracted spiral into heat death, how all said and done she was a shit of a human being, he a shit of a human being, and now he misses her so much, and now not at all, he can hardly bring to mind her face these days, can he, how did—and the understanding tearing through him: So the cosmos contains the possibility of feeling *that?* I want it so bad. I want it all. And I never want any of it ever again, those countless people who have left me in their wakes, those countless people I have left in mine.

It's 1978, 1981, 1985, all at once, and each time the man is in a different hotel bed with the same groupie, Nigel Taylor, peeled out of his skintight blue jeans and black leather jacket with matching riveted wristbands who, no matter when it is, looks seventeen and smells like patchouli. The first time they have it off Nigel sports Debbie Harry's two-tone rocker hair, the second Suzi Quatro's streaked brunette feathering, the third Cher's jet-black lion's mullet. Nigel has been in love with David Bowie since he was thirteen, growing up in Lambeth, and his friend Lace Nelson with the red Irish face and cutest green wool cowl-neck brought over *Diamond Dogs* one day after school, because it is evident to Nigel that David Bowie can read his thoughts, that they inhabit the same infrared fields of communion. Now he saves any extra cash he can from work at the car-rental agency in Hammersmith so he can fly to David's concerts whenever, wherever they are in the UK or Europe, and every once in a long while he can ease up to the lip of the stage, just like Bowie did with the Velvet Underground that night seven years earlier, ten years, fourteen, to make sure David can see him singing along to all his lyrics. God, his lyrics.

They are crushing. They laser right through your being. And if Nigel is lucky—and every once in a long while he is—David will lean over between songs to tell one of his hippopotamic security guards to invite him back to where David is staying after the show, and they will drink together, and giggle together, and David will be the personification of politeness, and eventually they will find themselves merging into a rainbow, and Nigel knows more than he has ever known anything in his entire life that David will grow to love him, too, given enough time, comprehend just how much they share, how one they honestly are in spirit, yet so far David can never seem to remember it isn't their first shag.

It is this flying, this tumbling faster and faster end over end through minus 454 degrees Fahrenheit and incandescent gas clouds and deep-space gales, those bangs on the nickel-steel-alloy capsule having moved from outside to inside until they are emanating from the core of the man's medulla, and yet it is also still 1993, now forty-six, him sitting across from Duncan at a table outside a café featuring Hungarian pastries on South Market Street in Wooster, Ohio, a five-minute drive from his son's campus, Duncan announcing he has decided to major in philosophy and the man's chest crowding with pride and light, look at what his son has grown into, look at that, Angie and he may not have gotten much right, but they got this dead-on, didn't they, even though it is still 1990, and the man is being shown his seat next to Iman at a dinner party, turning toward her, conjuring up one of his disarming grins, reaching out his hand by way of introduction, intensely aware he is no more to her than a manufactured character following his name, and she briefly extends her palm, and in that pause, drawn to her elegance, taken aback by how insistently his attention has settled upon her, somehow he already recognizes the fact that at the end of this evening he will invite her to tea tomorrow, nothing more, a plain gesture, gracious, friendly, even if it *is* still 2014, he back in the examination room, dressed in his street clothes, passing time with Coco until Dr. Soen returns from consulting with the radiologist.

Because, the man catches himself saying, apropos of nothing, people describe reading as a silent act, don't they.

Only you see it differently, says Coco.

It's very noisy. I mean, if you're doing it right. If you're using all your senses, only inside your head.

. . .

. . .

. . .

It is this relaxed extended silence between them, one that carries the decades they have crossed together.

Outside in the hall: indistinct voices, then the word *windshield*.

Coco pulls at her earlobe, says: I've never thought about it that way.

Reading, the man continues, you can actually feel yourself being thought by other people.

And you don't find that alarming.

You can feel yourself splitting into multiples.

And for you that's a calming emotion.

For me it's a fucking circus. He laughs. It's rush hour in a hurricane.

A rap at the door, Dr. Soen hustling through, lab coat swept back from beachball belly, dropping with a long exhalation into the seat across from the couple. He is winded. He is fixed. Leaning forward, palms on knees, he starts:

Okay. So. I should get right to the point, which I should tell you: I don't like what I'm seeing.

## THE HEART'S FILTHY LESSON

You quoting John Cage in *Silence* (1961), number twenty-seven on your reading list: *All I know about method is that when I am not working I sometimes think I know something, but when I am working, it is quite clear that I know nothing.*

You revealing to an always genial and intrigued Charlie Rose: *It's only when you start to move slightly out of your depth, and you feel you're a little bit lost . . . that's when you're going to get something exciting going. It'll either be a dismal failure or it will be spectacularly what you really want to do.*

Your biographer Wendy Leigh asserting you managed your bisexuality to get what you wanted.

Cyrinda Foxe, one of your stunning blond devotees (future wife of David Johansen of the New York Dolls, then Aerosmith's Steven Tyler) recounting: *Davy once called me into his hotel room from the bathroom to talk to him while he fucked a girl. He needed someone to talk to, and I guess that someone was me. I'd be watching TV and talking to David, and he'd be screwing some groupie. It was all very nonchalant.*

From number twenty-two on your reading list—Alfred Döblin's *Berlin Alexanderplatz* (1929): *I've made love to a lot of women, yet never one named Marie. But I'd like to.*

*Nobody wore the clothes he wore*, Mikal Gilmore writing in *Rolling Stone*, *princely yet feminine robes, tight pants that presented his sex as the center of his being.*

Bryan Wawzenek in *Ultimate Classic Rock* reviewing *Never Let Me Down* (1987): *There is no greater disappointment in Bowie's catalog than the nadir of what he later called his Phil Collins Years. This is just bad idea after bad idea: a self-serious concept piece about a glass spider, impersonations of John Lennon and Neil Young, a mid-song "rap" from Mickey Rourke, plus glossy production better suited to a Pepsi commercial.*

Bob Dylan meeting you for the first time at a party, turning to Ron Wood standing beside him, and asking loudly: *Who the fuck does this guy think he is?*

*Liminal Bowie posed at being a poseur*, biographer David Buckley offering, *made camouflage and misinformation part of his art.*

You proclaiming, your tone unclear—admiring, nostalgic, frank, ironic, provocative for provocation's sake: *Rock stars are fascists. Adolf Hitler was one of the first rock stars. Look at some of his films and see how he moved. I think he was quite as good as Jagger. The world will never see his like again.*

You confronting an unexpectedly discombobulated VJ Mark Goodman during a heretofore run-of-the-mill interview: *I'm floored by the fact that you have so few Black artists on MTV. Why is that? The only Black artists one does see are on about two-thirty in the morning to around six. Should it not be a challenge to make the media far more integrated?*

*It's on America's tortured brow*, you once singing, *that Mickey Mouse has grown up a cow.*

*Gloom is my default attitude*, you tendering.

*You've got to have an extreme right front come up and sweep everything off its feet and tidy everything up*, you professing, even as your fans scuttled to cover for you, claiming it was one more example of your cocaine psychosis talking.

*I'm always amazed that people take what I say seriously*, you remarking years later.

You getting a large tattoo, your only one, faded green on the back of your left calf, two years after meeting Iman, around the time you began referring to yourself as *a former drug addict*: a man with a frog in an extended palm riding a dolphin, surrounded by a variant of theologian Reinhold Niebuhr's 1951 Serenity Prayer translated into Katakana.

John Lennon reminiscing: *We seem to have had some communication together, but you never knew which David Bowie you were talking to.*

The dolphin a reference to Italian author Alberto Denti di Pirajno's *Grave for a Dolphin* (1956), about a young European traveler stranded in a Somalian village on the sea. By day he befriends a dolphin, at night falls in love with a beautiful, elusive woman who, he presumes, comes from said village. Unexpectedly, the woman disappears. Next morning the traveler discovers the dolphin having dragged itself across the sand and up to his hut to die peacefully near him. You track down a first edition and give it to Iman as a birthday present.

*I could have been Hitler in England,* you reflecting. *Wouldn't have been hard. Concerts alone got so enormously frightening that even the papers were saying "This ain't rock music, this is bloody Hitler! Something must be done!" And they were right. It was awesome. Actually, I wonder . . . I think I might have been a bloody good Hitler. I'd be an excellent dictator.*

Simon Reynolds in *Shock and Awe: Glam Rock and Its Legacy* (2016), arguing Buddhism's primary precepts stayed with you throughout your life: *Bowie said that the idea of transience never left him: the self as a figment, a will-o'-the-wisp illusion, the thinnest of membranes masking a profound emptiness. But in Buddhism this interior void is not troubling or nihilistic: the true self is the no-self. The self is a magic show, a trick done with mirrors.*

*I've been depressed plenty of times,* you explaining to a stringer, *but I've never actually been bored. Looking out a window and watching people is quite enough to keep me occupied for half an hour.*

From number ten on your reading list—Martin Amis's *Money* (1984): *It really takes it out of you, not knowing anything. You're given comedy and miss all the jokes. Sometimes, as I sit alone in my flat in London and stare out the window, I think how dismal it is, how heavy, to watch the rain and not know why it falls. Each life is a game of chess that went to hell on the seventh move.*

*It took me five years to become an overnight success*, you spelling out. *No one in music is given that kind of time these days. Think about what's been lost.*

*Fans allow aspects of Bowie's personality to spread into their own, either consciously or unconsciously*, David Buckley noting in *Strange Fascination* (1992). *Not only do they copy him stylistically, but they also copy his mannerisms from videos, memorize parts of interviews and repeat them as if they were their own thoughts, and model their likes and dislikes on his. A female fan simply says*: Basically, I tell strangers I'm a Bowie fan and then clam up. I feel I've told them my station in life and everything about me in those four words.

Paul Mathur in *Melody Maker's* reviewing *Oy Veh Baby* (1992), Tin Machine's concert album: *This is the moment where finally, categorically and, let's face it, lumpily, he ceases to exist as an artist of any worth whatsoever. It's not the glamorous plane crash, not even any sort of paid-his-due dying candle . . . . It's not just dying, it's ensuring posterity will never know he existed.*

*I'm the last person to pretend that I'm a radio*, you submitting. *I'd rather go out and be a color television set.*

*I'm a pioneer*, you proffering, *and pioneers, as they say, get all the arrows.*

*Almost every singer with a hit record today is the bankruptcy of to-morrow*, opining William Krsilovsky, a lawyer specializing in copyright law.

From number twelve on your reading list—Gustave Flaubert's *Madame Bovary* (1856): *You forget everything. The hours slip by. You travel in your chair through centuries you seem to see before you, your thoughts are caught up in the story, dallying with the details or follow-ing the course of the plot, you enter into characters, so that it seems as if it were your own heart beating beneath their costumes.*

*David Bowie the "out" gay was just another role for Bowie, who wasn't, of course, even David Bowie, really, but David Jones of south London playing at being a media star called David Bowie*, John Gill surmising in *Queer Noises* (1995). *While Bowie long ago dropped the pretense of even bisexuality, an aura of queerness has clung to him to the extent that he is probably the only heterosexual*

*on the planet who has so much space dedicated to him in the world's gay media.*

⋆⋆

*At bottom,* you acknowledging, *I am a collector.*

⋆⋆

And elsewhere: *I'm really just my own little corporation of characters.*

⋆⋆

From number forty-nine on your reading list—Richard Wright's *Black Boy* (1945): *It was not a matter of believing or disbelieving what I read, but of feeling something new, of being affected by something that made the look of the world different.*

⋆⋆

One night the operatic Angie throwing herself down the stairs in a jealous fury, and you stepping gingerly over her on your way out the door, saying over your shoulder: *Well, when you feel like it, and if you're not dead, call me.*

⋆⋆

*I reinvented my image so many times,* you confessing, *that I'm in denial I was originally an overweight Korean woman.*

⋆⋆

*Religion,* you advancing, *is for people who fear hell. Spirituality is for people who have been there.*

92

The Catholic League for Religious and Civil Rights calling the video for "The Next Day," that one in which you portray Christ in an S&M bar named (nodding to Boccaccio's collection of tales told by a group sheltering from the black death in a secluded villa outside Florence) the Decameron, the *work of a switch-hitting, bisexual senior citizen from London; in short, the video reflects the artist—it is a mess.*

*A cop knelt and kissed the feet of a priest,* you singing, *and a queer threw up at the sight of that.*

You quoting John Cage in *Silence* (1961): *Disharmony, to paraphrase Bergson's statement about disorder, is simply a harmony to which many are unaccustomed.*

*With a suit,* you advising a journalist, *always wear big British shoes, the ones with large welts. There's nothing worse than dainty little Italian jobs at the end of the leg line.*

Ava Cherry recalling that time you went to visit Paul and Linda McCartney at the Plaza in New York: *They just sat looking at us. David asked Paul a question. Linda answered. David asked a second question and Linda answered again. David said to him:* You can't speak for yourself? *Paul said something smart and David looked at me and said:* We're going. *And we got up and walked out.*

You and Iman participating in the late nineties in 7th on Sale, which supports research into HIV/AIDS.

*Our parents' generation has lost control, given up,* you spelling out to yet another interviewer. *They're scared of the future. My generation is going to make an even greater mess of it. There can only be disaster ahead.*

You and Iman giving to 21st Century Leaders (gathering artworks from movers and shakers in all fields to raise funds for various charitable causes), Every Mother Counts (advocacy and mobilization campaign to increase education and funding for maternal and child health), Food Bank For New York City (distribution of donations from manufacturers, wholesalers, retailers, and government agencies to organizations providing free food to the city's hungry), Keep A Child Alive (providing antiretroviral treatment to African kids and their families with HIV/AIDS) . . . u.s.w.

You telling an interviewer in Sweden in 1976: *I believe Britain could benefit from a Fascist leader* and, six days later, upon your return to London from Berlin ("China Girl" [1983]: *I stumble into town just like a sacred cow, visions of swastikas in my head,*

*plans for everyone*), dressed as a version of the Thin White Duke (modeled on the Aryan *Übermensch*), giving a Nazi salute from the back of a black open-top Mercedes Benz limo before thousands of cheering fans at Victoria Station.

*Speak in extremes*, you recommending. *It'll save you time.*

David Buckley grumbling in *Strange Fascination: Fans have had to endure "Heroes" being used in TV adverts for the likes of Kodak, Microsoft, CGU (pensions/investments and insurance), and, in 2004, in an actually rather good instrumental version by Nathan Larson, Wanadoo. This fan, for one, has never felt at all heroic when Microsoft Windows flashes up for the umpteenth time:* This program has performed an illegal operation and will be shut down—invalid fault in KERNEL32.DLL. *Nor does the idea of investing in a pension come across as even mildly evocative of the Dunkirk spirit.*

From number eighteen on your reading list—Greil Marcus's *Mystery Train: Images of America in Rock 'n' Roll Music* (1975): *Blues grew out of the need to live in the brutal world that stood ready in ambush the moment one walked out of the church.*

*Rock is only a conveyer of information now*, you proposing. *It's not a conveyer of rebellion. There has been a breakdown personified by the rave culture of the nineties, where the audience became at least as*

*important as whoever was playing. It's almost like the artist is just there to accompany the audience in what the audience is doing.*

Bono estimating: *Bowie was probably the last rock star I could believe in, because after him came punk, and then we weren't allowed to believe in rock stars anymore.*

*My-my, someone fetch a priest,* you singing, *you can't say no to the beauty and the beast.*

*The depressing realization in this age of dumbing down,* you complaining, *is that the questions have moved from* Was Nietzsche right about God? *to* How big was his dick?

Aaron Lariviere in *Stereogum* reviewing *Tonight* (1984): *Listening to David Bowie should not be a painful experience, yet here we are. The record that preceded this one,* Let's Dance, *was perfectly listenable, fun as hell, and admittedly dumb.* Tonight *was crapped out in the wake of that infinitely superior album's success, and it feels like it. The downside to the superstardom that accompanied hits like "Let's Dance" and "Modern Love" is a new generation of fans tuning into Bowie's music, fans who neither know nor care about his Berlin period, Ziggy, the Thin White Duke, or any of it . . . . It's hard to recommend* Tonight *for anything besides morbid curiosity.*

You admitting: *I find the idea of having to say I'm a musician in any way an embarrassment to me because I don't really believe that. I don't believe I'm very accomplished at music. I give a little sigh of relief when I come up with something that sounds whole and complete and functions as a piece of music. I'm far more interested in the blending of different things. I have the attention span of a grasshopper, which means it's very difficult for me to become a craftsman. I suppose I'm quite promiscuous . . . artistically speaking, of course. Monogamy and me . . . we've always been just like* this.

*He left Terry in a mental home for nineteen years without sending a penny for his private treatment,* your mother's sister Pat protesting. *Terry was handsome, charming, and intelligent, but when he fell ill David didn't want to know, because it was a reminder that the same thing could happen to him because it ran in the family.*

You and Iman giving to Mercury Phoenix Trust (subsidizing over seven hundred projects across the globe to assist in the fight against HIV/AIDS), Mines Advisory Group (clearing remnants of conflict from the world's poorest nations while educating and employing local people), Save the Children (focusing on abuse, HIV/AIDS, disaster relief, education, poverty), Witness (using online technologies to open the eyes of the world to human rights violations) . . . u.s.w.

***

Rumors circulating to this day that, as you and photographer Andy Kent drive down Entlastungsstrasse along the Berlin Wall in 1976 and pass the blown-up hill marking the site of Hitler's bunker, you give a Nazi salute. Kent allegedly snaps your picture, which you make him swear never to release without your permission. Kent keeps his word.

*I think the biggest frightener now*, you inveighing, *is the disturbing lack of interest among a certain proportion of young people–a certain lack of interest in . . . no curiosity about what's going on.* It's the *fashionable dumbing down of a generation. Even as a teenager, I used to get really pissed off when people were purposefully dumb. I fell out with many musicians for the same reason.* Oh, don't need to. Don't want to. I was like, Well, then, go away.

From number seventy-two on your reading list—Nathanael West's *Day of the Locust* (1939): *Their boredom becomes more and more terrible. They realize that they've been tricked and burn with resentment. Every day of their lives they read the newspapers and went to the movies. Both fed them on lynchings, murder, sex crimes, explosions, wrecks, love nests, fires, miracles, revolutions, war. This daily diet made sophisticates of them. The sun is a joke. Nothing can ever be violent enough to make taut their slack minds and bodies.*

*I don't know where I'm going from here*, you propounding, *but I promise it won't be boring.*

Cherry Vanilla, punk singer and publicist known for her outrageous marketing strategies—including, e.g., an open offer to perform oral sex on any DJ who would play your records—recounting: *David and I were planning an album together called* Electric Beatnik, *which was going to be a mix of his synthesizer music and my poetry. We talked a lot about it on the phone, and then in person in Canada, and then a friend was throwing a cocaine party for him in New York and we were both there. I mentioned the album to him. He said something to me in German and walked away. And that's the last time I spoke to him.*

From number twelve on your reading list—Gustave Flaubert's *Madame Bovary* (1856), redux: *At the bottom of her heart, she was waiting for something to happen. Like shipwrecked sailors, she turned despairing eyes upon the solitude of her life, seeking afar off some white sail in the mists of the horizon. She did not know what this chance would be . . . . but each morning, as she awoke, she hoped it would come that day; she listened to every sound, sprang up with a start, wondered that it did not come; then at sunset, always more saddened, she longed for the morrow.*

*Remembering,* you submitting, *is an act of defiance.*

*David didn't like confrontation,* Angie Bowie recollecting. *He didn't care for it at all. He would always rather leave. It was pointless*

*trying to fight with him, as it was like fighting with a blancmange.*
*There was no resistance. You felt like you were torturing a child.*

⋆⋆

*Our culture believes it can Botox its pain away*, you observing.

⋆⋆

You donating royalties from the second single off *Black Tie White Noise* (1993), your first album after marrying Iman, to Unity Hall, a former crack house in LA's South Central, to help Arsenio Hall convert it into a youth center.

⋆⋆

From number twelve on your reading list redux—Gustave Flaubert's *Madame Bovary* (1856), re-redux: *Never touch your idols: the gilding will stick to your fingers.*

⋆⋆

From number forty-two on your reading list—F. Scott Fitzgerald's *The Great Gatsby* (1925): *Reserving judgments is a matter of infinite hope.*

⋆⋆

*This ain't rock 'n' roll*, you shouting at the start of *Diamond Dogs* (1974)—*this is* GENOCIDE.

⋆⋆

Yoko Ono recollecting: *After John died, David was always there for Sean and me. When Sean was at boarding school in Switzerland,*

100

*David would pick him up and take him on trips to museums and let Sean hang out at his recording studio in Geneva.*

*I would love to have been like Sting and been a teacher,* you surprising Charlie Rose by saying when he asks you what you would have been if not a rock star. *What really gets me off is to be able to introduce people to new things that make them excited. You know, opening up some worlds. I remember when people did that for me. I always felt it was a gift when anybody took me anywhere.*

Bill Wyman in *Entertainment* reviewing *Tin Machine II* (1991): *Some people think David Bowie was the Madonna of the seventies, but the comparison only reveals the limitations of both artists. Madonna, of course, could never hope to approach the dizzying musical and thematic changes Bowie has made effortlessly over the years, from androgynous glam sensation (Ziggy Stardust) to Philly Soul man (Young Americans) to chart-topping pop beast for the eighties (Let's Dance). And Bowie, no piker when it comes to manipulating his image for commercial benefit, nonetheless lacks Madonna's epic abilities in these areas, and perhaps as a result has never made his mark on the zeitgeist to the extent she has. Tin Machine's 1989 self-titled first album went nowhere. Everything on* Tin Machine II *from its enigmatic lyrics (When the kiss of the comb tears my face from the bone) to its blithely varied music (blues, art rock, hard rock, schmaltz) and tepid melodies (Bowie's songwriting muse has largely left him)–sounds like typically mediocre late-period David Bowie.*

Bob Geldof recounting how you agreed to participate in Band Aid to raise funds for the Ethiopian disaster: *We showed him famine footage cut to the Cars' song "Drive." Bowie sat there in tears and said* Right, I'm giving up a song. *I said* Hang on . . . *I didn't want David giving up a fucking song. But of course he was right. That was the moment people said,* Fuck everything. Take whatever you want from me. *And it took a David Bowie to make that call.*

You quoting John Cage in *Silence* (1961): *I went to a concert upstairs in Town Hall. The composer whose works were being performed had provided program notes. One of these notes was to the effect that there is too much pain in the world. After the concert I was walking along with the composer and he was telling me how the performances had not been quite up to snuff. So I said,* Well, I enjoyed the music, but I don't agree with that program note about there being too much pain in the world. *He said,* What? Don't you think there's enough? *I said* I think there's just the right amount.

*Confront a corpse at least once,* you encouraging. *The unmitigated absence of life is the most disturbing and challenging confrontation you will ever have.*

*Whenever I heard someone say something intelligent,* you acknowledging, *I used it later as if it were my own. When I saw a quality in someone that I liked, I took it. I still do that all the time. It's just like a car, man, replacing parts.*

And elsewhere: *I am responsible for starting a whole new school of pretension.*

*I think Mick Jagger would be astounded and amazed if he realized that to many people he is not a sex symbol,* you asserting, *but a mother image.*

*I don't think Mick is evil at all,* you adding elsewhere. *He represents the sort of harmless, bourgeois kind of evil that one can accept with a shrug.*

*It would be my guess that Madonna is not a very happy woman,* you point-of-facting. *From my own experience that kind of clawing need to be the center of attention is not a pleasant place to be.*

From number seventy-nine on your reading list—John Dos Passos's *The 42ⁿᵈ Parallel* (1930): *U. S. A. is a group of holding companies, some aggregations of trade unions, a set of laws bound in calf, a radio network, a chain of moving picture theatres, a column of stock quotations rubbed out and written in by a Western Union boy on a blackboard, a public library full of old newspapers and dogeared history books with protests scrawled on the margins in pencil. U. S. A. is a lot of men buried in their uniforms in Arlington Cemetery.*

*I'm afraid of Americans,* you singing. *God is an American.*

*I'm an instant superstar,* you explaining. *Just add water and stir.*

Tyler Clark's two-line review of *Hours* (1999) in *Medium*: *Bowie just phoned in this one. It isn't bad, because it isn't anything.*

From number six on your reading list—Yukio Mishima's *The Sailor Who Fell from Grace with the Sea* (1963): *A father is a reality-concealing machine.*

To compose "Fame," which became your first number one single on US Billboard Hot 100, displacing Glen Campbell's "Rhinestone Cowboy," it taking you and John Lennon exactly forty-five minutes.

*Fame itself,* you acknowledging, *doesn't really afford you anything more than a good seat in a restaurant.*

*The truth of course is that there is no journey,* you summing up. *We are arriving and departing all at the same time.*

$$\overset{*}{\phantom{x}}\overset{}{*}\,{*}$$

*Well, I'm almost an atheist,* you confiding. *Just give me a couple months.*

$$\overset{*}{\phantom{x}}{*}\,{*}$$

*When I'm stuck for a closing to a lyric,* you tongue-in-cheeking, *I will drag out my last resort: overwhelming illogic.*

$$\overset{*}{\phantom{x}}{*}\,{*}$$

*I'm looking for backing for an unauthorized autobiography that I'm writing,* you ironizing. *Hopefully, this will sell in such huge numbers that I'll be able to sue myself for an extraordinary amount of money and finance the film version in which I'll play everybody.*

**HEROES**

Because listen to "Heroes" more determinedly than you've listened to it before. Because in the dark. Because a still room. Because lying down, eyes shut, headphones. Because you will hear how Bowie gets going by laying down a backing track without form, without melody, without lyrics, without vocal, without name. Because George Murray on base warped with flanger; Carlos Alomar on guitar; Dennis Davis on drums, kick, snare, tom-toms; far, far down in the mix, barely perceptible, Bowie playing piano; and off in the corner Brian Eno with his EMS VCS 3 briefcase synthesizer birthing celestial ether. Because on another track Bowie caressing another synthesizer, a pulsing ARP Solina. Because a week later he invites Robert Fripp into the studio to overlay three feedbacky guitar riffs run through Eno's synthesizer. Because Bowie adds a brass track by pumping chords through an electro-mechanical mellotron and, when he can't find the cowbell he wants lying around in the studio, asks Visconti to tink out the beat with a fork on a metal tape reel while Bowie himself tambourines to keep the song's momentum rolling forward. Because only after that, a final gesture, do the lyrics and melody come to him. Because Visconti sets up three mics to record Bowie's voice, one directly in front of him, one twenty feet away, and one fifty, each fitted with an electronic gate tripped depending on how loud Bowie sings, simultaneously creating a breathy, intimate and echoey, roomy sound. Because on the last track backing vocals, Visconti's Brooklyn accent aligning with Bowie's English. Because that's why.

## EVERYBODY SAYS HI

Testing one, two . . . ha. We good? Sure. Take your time. I'll just blather on while you— Um, let's see. I'm Angie Bowie. I grew up on Cyprus. My dad was a colonel in the US Army. Mining engineer.

. . . ?

That's where I went to school—Cyprus. There, Switzerland, and London. And those couple months at Connecticut College when I was sixteen until, you know, I slept with this incredibly sexy girl and they expelled me. Which I guess leaves little doubt I was raised Roman Catholic. (Laughs.)

. . . ?

David? He wasn't raised much of anything. He quickly learned to question organized religion. Unfortunately, it took him quite a bit longer to learn how to question disorganized ones. Do you think I might be able to get a cup of coffee?

. . . ?

Lovely. Black. A little sugar. You're a sweetheart.

. . . ?

Um, let's see. I've been a model, an actress, and an author. I've sung some, too. A lot of people don't know that. They should check out my album *Moon Goddess*.

. . . ?

*Lipstick Legends: When Boys Became Girls.* Memoir about what the seventies felt like to somebody who lived in the midst of them. I hope we'll get to talk about it, too. Uh, what else? I've got this really good head for business. *Really* good. I mean, look at my ex. (Laughs.)

. . . ?

I've been married once, lived with Andy Lipka for three years, back when he was Drew Blood, three and change, and I've been with Michael since, what, 1993. Oh, and I appeared on *Celebrity Big Brother* recently—so you know I must be famous.

... ?

Son with David. Daughter with Drew—Stacia. Lovely girl. But not so much into the mother thing, to be honest.

... ?

God. The smells alone. The shit, both physical and emotional. I quite prefer cats.

... ?

Sure. Okay. Let's go.

... ?

Thanks so much for having me on today. It's wonderful to be here.

... ?

Oh, god. I have no interest at all in slander. None. Seriously. I hate that sort of idiot pettiness. It's cheerleaders snapping in hallways between classes. Do we *ever* outgrow high school? So I have to be careful not to get caught up in this vortex of dumb anecdotes. I don't want to put you at the mercy of the same stories I'm always pressed to tell. I'm—think of me as a kind of witness, okay? An historian. You could say I was in the trenches back then. I want to tell people who might be interested a little more about what it was like down there. What *he* was really like. I mean, people get things into their heads. They glorify those things. Only let me tell you: whatever you're imagining? It wasn't that. No Promised Land. No Sodom and Gomorrah. It was more like, uh, that stretch of New Jersey across the George Washington Bridge. (Laughs.)

. . . ?

Let me put it this way. The Brits talked about the Cypriots as if the people on the island were outsiders in their own country. And, even though I was born there, both my parents were American. So I was American. Except I wasn't. I was a foreigner even in the land of my birth. Which means crap like country, nationalism, that rubbish? It doesn't matter to me. It honestly doesn't. I've always preferred the feeling of living between places. Between ideas, genders, geographies. It keeps you chirpy. Easy is easy, of course, but it has nothing to do with living. You might as well take a long nap or get married.

. . . ?

My accent? I can't seem to shake my London years, I suppose.

. . . ?

Nineteen sixty-seven. I'd just arrived. Imagine this starry-eyed girl all of eighteen attending Kingston Polytechnic in marketing and economics. Long story short, I soon got involved with a record executive who shall remain nameless. Calvin Mark Lee. I thought he was an elderly man. He must have been pushing thirty. One evening Calvin brings me to one of David's concerts. This is when David was still with Feathers and all over himself about Hermione—

. . . ?

Hemione Farthingale. Right. She played guitar. Theirs was
the kind of romantic tosh that would make a full-grown elephant chunder. Anyway, we talked after the show, the four of
us, and over the next few weeks David and I got to know each
other a bit. When Hermione kicked him out—well, she simply
hit the ejector button. No warning whatsoever. David never
saw it coming, even though she must have been planning her
breakout for some time. So he was utterly gutted. He actually
got sick—as in quite physically ill. He crawled under the covers
and wouldn't come out. One day he calls me up and asks me
over to take care of him.

. . . ?

He was like that.

. . . ?

Yes.

. . . ?

Where's my mummy? Exactly.

. . . ?

Oh, well, being with David was the equivalent of tending to a
needy two-year-old. Twenty-four seven. At that point in his life,
if one were to have made a film, it would portray him sitting in
front of the camera for ninety minutes shouting *Look at me! Look
at me! Look at me!* I suppose in a sense that never changed.

. . . ?

It was the sort of relationship that defines the rest of your life. I won't lie. I knew I had found someone without equal in him. Someone different and difficult and great in so many ways. One in a million, you know? That immediate mitochondrial connection. It seemed as if we had known each other forever already, like we were simply meeting up after having been apart.

. . . ?

I was up front with him from the outset. I told him all I wanted to do was work as an actress and director in London. I thought for sure I'd make my name as a scriptwriter one day. David was all about that. He was unbelievably supportive. You know, rhetorically speaking. Ha. And so not long after we met I presented him with a deal: If you want, I told him, I can help you. I can market your product. I'm good at that. We can make things happen. We can make a name for you. There I was, eighteen, nineteen, fresh in London, spouting such unmitigated drivel. In retrospect, it's quite hilarious, isn't it. And there David was, only twenty or something like that, believing all it took to be a star was wanting to be a star. We didn't know from bollocks. Our mission in life was to redefine self-absorption on a daily basis. We excelled.

. . . ?

I'll help you get your career started, I said to him, then you help me do what I want to do. David leapt at the idea. We developed a plan, followed it, modified it, cocked up, went back to the drawing board, plowed on. Our secret was to never even consider giving up. We had a goal and we were going to do what it took to reach it.

. . . ?

I made a home for us. That's what I did. I anchored us as a couple. I was everything to David: creative partner, lover, soul mate. Don't get me wrong. Our day-to-day could be fraught. He could be aloof. Remote. Short-tempered. Moody. Frosty, even. And needless to say astronomically narcissistic. You should see the odd wobbly he could throw. He was a sulker. Stubborn. Unable to share. Impatient. Over the next few months he gradually changed. He really did. He warmed to me. I mean, we always got along famously, even when we didn't. Even our fights felt just right.

. . . ?

Let's face it: I took fucking incredible care of him. I *babysat* him, for Christ's sake. I made him feel important and loved. You know, what every toddler wants. He wrote the "The Prettiest Star" for me as a kind of thanks. *You will be my rest and peace, child. You and I will rise up all the way. All because of what you are.* Quote, unquote. It was really quite touching.

. . . ?

My background in theater? I used it to style him. From day one. The Ziggy Stardust red hair? That came from paging through back copies of *Vogue* together. The Aladdin Sane makeup? The "Space Oddity" costumes? We worked on those side by side.

. . . ?

I've got to tell you—his voice? His music? This may piss some people off, but back then he sounded only okay. There was nothing singular about his songs or the way he sang them. Have you heard his first album? Q.E.D. And it was released on the very same day—June 1, 1967—as *Sgt. Pepper*. Awesome timing. Real head for business. Ha. So I got to thinking, and one day I said to him: You know, David, I don't want to bruise your ego or anything, but you sound exactly like everybody else right now—I mean, except for "Space Oddity," which was this gimmick song anyway. Even Tony—Tony Visconti—Tony wouldn't touch it. He thought "Space Oddity" trite at best, a bit of a damp squib at worst, so he gave it to Gus Dudgeon to produce. But even when it hit, and the band started to tour for real? Even then it wasn't like David suddenly got discovered. He simply got a bit more airtime. Everyone assumed "Space Oddity" was a one off. He'd had his fifteen minutes, thank you very much. The fame—that whole thing took another year or two.

. . . ?

My idea. Damn straight. I tell the band: Listen, guys: you've *got* to do more than sing. Singing isn't cutting it for you. A look. Let's develop a look. They agreed—warily at first, mind you; very, very warily. I took it upon myself to outfit them. They became my little sweet dress-up dolls. I was naturally chuffed. We went around London to various shops asking the owners for the most outrageous stuff they had. You know, the sort they kept in the back room for fear of what the result would be if

113

they put it on show in the windows. David saw the fancy dresses. It was girl-crush. He had the perfect figure for them, and they were truly spectacular—eighteenth-century opulence. My idea was easy: You wear the blinding clothes of a rock star, you eventually become a blinding rock star. I essentially began to manage their shows as well. "Five Years"? I asked David to write that, to give you a case in point. I knew we needed something rousing, this apocalyptic anthem to end each evening. The audience always looked like they were ready to come, but there was no way to get them over the top. If they could just sing along to a catchy chorus about the end of the world—

. . . ?

Oh, you know. They were about being fuck-the-world-I'm-all-alienated-and-deep-so-I-dye-my-hair-red-and-paint-my-face-blue-just-like-everybody-else. So much like each other they thought themselves individuals. Sweet, injured, gullible.

. . . ?

I was the one who urged David to sell the outcast as lifestyle. Break down gender borders, too. That was me. Gay, straight, didn't know, didn't matter. That way *all* the freaks would want to come out to see David's shows and dance to his music and relish the experience of him because everybody felt personally invited and welcome at a time when mainstream music was letting fall between the fiscal cracks huge portions of the culturally dispossessed. Does that sound crass? I can't be arsed with that way of thinking. David had this uncanny intuitive ability to make everybody feel like he was speaking to them and no one else. He made them feel part of something bigger when they had never felt like part of anything in their lives—yet made them feel like the thing they were part of was about being tip-to-toe singular and appreciated. It was so beautiful to see. Come unto me, my aberrations. We needed to learn how to tap that, and then—*bam*: one day everything clicked. The band started getting better. *Really* better. We had finally figured out how to expand our marketing base.

. . . ?

"The Prettiest Star" was for me. "Kooks" he wrote for Duncan and me both. "Golden Years" was my present because I'd done so well on the *Mike Douglas Show.*

. . . ?

Nineteen seventy-five, I think. 1975 or 1976. I sang "I Got a Crush on You"—my first singing gig, and there I was in front of like forty million people. David loved it. He thought I was brilliant. So he wrote "Golden Years" for me and rung me up in the middle of the night—I can't remember where he was—maybe Berlin—I don't remember—and sang it to me over the phone. *I'll stick with you, baby, for a thousand years. Nothing's gonna touch you in these golden years.* He always knew how to undo me, even as we both knew there was no way what we had was going to last.

. . . ?

*Run for the shadows?* Fuck if I know. Listen. Let me tell you something. *Everybody* reads all this codswallop into David's lyrics. Like the words are some huge graduate seminar on existentialism and the Meaning of Life. Sorry to disappoint, but you know why David really wrote his songs? David really wrote his songs so he didn't have to talk. He wrote his songs so he didn't have to explain what he was feeling to anyone who actually mattered to him. He usually threw shit onto a piece of paper and saw what stuck. He didn't use cut-ups because he was some sort of Burroughsesque genius. He used cut-ups because most of the time he couldn't come up with anything intelligent to say himself. The tune was always far more significant to him. Words were there for no reason other than that there had to be something to pin the melody onto.

. . . ?

That's why songwriters write songs. I hope this doesn't come as a big shock to anyone. They write songs because they're inarticulate and unable to communicate any kind of real emotion to another human being. And then you're supposed to be soooooo delighted when you're able to piece together some fragment of perhaps some vague version of what they might have meant. It's like middle-school poetry. *Oh, I'm being soooooo profound!* David's songs were a secret code even he had no idea how to crack. They were a mask he put on that allowed him to streak through packed soccer stadiums without being recognized.

. . . ?

*Claimed* they were for me. I'm sure he meant it when he wrote them, but you have to understand—that was just to make points with me on a particular day. This was a side of David his fans could never get. The media either. David had this—I don't know—this magic power. He could endear himself to people so they couldn't help loving him and working hard to promote him.

. . . ?

He lived every second of his life for acclaim while pretending it was merely this unexpected, unwanted byproduct of his oh-so-authentic-and-eccentric cutting-edge art. Like he would produce that art whether or not he got the veneration. Bollocks. Everything he did he did to be adored. That's neither good nor bad. I'm not judging. It's simply how it was. Anyway, hey, I wasn't prepared to let such rabid need on his part destroy a perfectly good business relationship. His music and his sexuality were the currencies David had available to him to get what he wanted. My job was to help him exploit both.

. . . ?

Really? Does that still get people worked up? I thought by now *everybody* knew we had an open marriage. David had been up front about it with me from the start. He told me in no uncertain terms before we were married that he didn't love me. He used those very words. *I don't love you.* Me, on the other hand, I loved him terribly. Monstrously. What are you going to do? He warned me not to expect anything conventional from him because, he said, it simply wasn't how he was put together. I got that. I did. And it was fine by me. David was like no one else I had ever met, and this was the price to pay to have him. It was either that or no David at all, and I couldn't conceive of such a thing. It would have been like trying to imagine infinity. Most people might not agree, to which I say: Fuck you kindly. You had to be around him to understand. He was my one and only. The turd. (Laughs.)

. . . ?

Of *course* it hurt. I mean, it hurt and, um, it didn't. It hurts and it doesn't. I knew very well what I was getting myself into. I was a big girl. Even as I hoped against hope I could change the algebra. I was young, but I wasn't, you know, all fur coat and no knickers.

. . . ?

The bottom line is we agreed to marry primarily to prevent me from being deported from England. How could I have managed his career from the States or wherever? It didn't make any sense. Otherwise the word *marriage* probably wouldn't have entered our vocabulary.

. . . ?

Hell, no. I didn't turn a blind eye to his let's call them comprehensive explorations into the art of fucking. Just the opposite. I *helped* him. I aided and abetted. I was very good at it, too, if I do say so myself. I rounded up free-spirited girls and boys for his pleasure. I brought them home and we luxuriated in them together. Let me just add, in case it isn't clear: I had my proper and delicious share of them as well. It was who we were. You could call ours a marriage of luxurious inconvenience.

. . . ?

Yeah, that one's true. We got married in, what was it, March, 1970. We went shopping for a nice dress the day before. On our way home, we decided to drop in on a woman artist friend to say hi. Well, somehow one thing led to another and we ended up in bed with her. The result was we were late for our own wedding the next morning.

. . . ?

God no. We didn't think twice about it. Why should we think twice about it? Everything back then was universal spiritual love, and by universal spiritual love we meant raw mindless sex with clouds of jasmine incense.

. . . ?

Weeks after our wedding David fell for Laurita Watson. You remember her?

. . . ?

Nobody does. She was this knockout Black ex-madam from Harlem who came to London to open a restaurant. David and she were—holy god. They had a yearlong fling while we were busy navigating our new whatever you want to call it. For most of that time Laurita lived with us in our flat. It made me feel good because it made David feel good. The whole thing was positively bizarre and divine.

. . . ?

I'd, uh, I guess I'd explain it this way: David and I simply lived within a different reality matrix from most people. So. Fucking. What. How the herd mooed didn't concern us in the least. Have you ever noticed, when it comes to relationships, those of a let's call it politically correct persuasion are appallingly parochial? It's my deep conviction they need to get out more. Fact is an insult to their self-righteous monotony and lack of moral, social, and psychological complexity. Can you tell I get cheesed off easily about such complete bullshit?

. . . ?

You have to understand something, I'd tell them. A man who has an affair can genuinely, profoundly love both women in his life at once, even as those women can genuinely, profoundly love him. Ditto if you flip the sexes. Why is that so hard for the prats to grasp? At the end of the day, it's all about experiential bandwidth.

. . . ?

No, no. Truth never appears in the singular, does it, not after you're five or six years old and first learn Santa-god is simply one in a long string of lies your parents and society will tell you. After that, the notion of an unconditional certainty goes away, except for academics and other fundamentalists. The realization is as freeing as it is terrifying.

. . . ?

What David and I had never upset me or made me feel disrespected or neglected. Actually, I think Laurita was closer to me than she was to him. She was a great person. And may I add hot as hell.

. . . ?

That makes David sound like he was somehow more or less faithful to a handful of people at the time—a serial polygamist. But let me paint you a larger picture. We named the focal point of our flat the Pit. It was this four-foot-deep hole in our sitting room filled with a fur-lined bed. The innumerable permutations of sexuality were explored there, frequently, in rigorous and stupendous detail, in front of various audiences, many of whose members ended up participating in the festivities as the night and the drugs flowed on.

. . . ?

Everyone believed exchanging bodily fluids in diverse ways had something to do with the notion of freedom. Looking back, I get that attitude a bit less every day. But still. Everybody had a *brilliant* time. I suppose these days the piously pure would slap some banal label on the enterprise—sex positive or some such rubbish. How I would phrase it is that we had some of the most *amaaaazing* orgies at Oakley Street. Period. Oh. My. God. Fucking *amaaaazing.* My only stipulations were that no one got fucked in private and everyone acknowledged me as queen. David happily agreed. Everything had to be a communal effort, like living theater or going to church. And let me tell you, David made a stellar religion out of the bonk. He was our bisexual alley-cat pope.

. . . ?

That's the thing, right? There was another side to all this. David was wont to search out people—whether it was simply for a leg over or to collaborate with in other more sophisticated ways—who weren't his equals. That's how he got what he wanted. He used them in a constant quest for that love and adoration we were talking about. I don't think he fully found it until Iman came along. Let me say, though, in no equivocal terms: Iman is no angel.

. . . ?

Let's just leave it at that, shall we?

. . . ?

David and I weren't living in some utopian commune. There was nothing idealistic and very little communal about it. That foaming-at-the-mouth life comes at a price. And how. Part of it involves the elementary process of growing up. Part involves burning out. Part involves the increasing tedium of repetition masquerading as novelty. And part involves—how to say it?—involves merely wanting to be conscious when you're conscious, if that makes sense.

. . . ?

How long were David and I happy? I don't honestly remember—three or maybe four out of those ten years? Something like that. We became unhappy, or at least I did, when the areas of his life he had stopped sharing with me were no longer joyous for either of us. By the early seventies, he had entered a long, sad, slow-motion pileup that would last a bloody decade.

. . . ?

Where to begin? There were so many wee hours I found myself holding David up in the middle of some godforsaken street
while he puked all over his own shoes.

. . . ?

He became thoroughly pathetic. And that was nothing com-
pared to what went down when he began traveling without
me.

. . . ?

I was summoned across the globe to save him on countless
occasions. Four or five flights later there I was cleaning up
after him. There was this time, you know, he was living in
LA and I was living in New York. A panic-stricken phone
call in the middle of the night. David wouldn't or couldn't
tell me what was wrong. He just kept babbling on the other
end of the line about how I had to fly out straightaway to be
with him. He was genuinely scared to death of something.
You could hear it. So I jumped on the next plane, flew across
the country, dashed to the Beverly Hills Hotel where he was
staying, talked the guy at the front desk into giving me a key
to his room, walked in—and found him in the midst of fucking what's-her-name, Claudia Lennear, that soul singer. He
looks over his shoulder at me and says all sheepishly: Oops.
Sorry, luv.

. . . ?

I closed the door and beelined directly for the bar so they could finish in peace while I got legless.

. . . ?

This other time? He's still busy coming apart in LA. By now I had probably moved back to London. Anyway, there he is, ringing me up yet again in the middle of the night, claiming he's being held captive by a warlock and two witches. I kid you not. Satan, he said, was on his way from the swimming pool as we spoke. He could hear the Lord of Darkness rummaging around in the hall outside his door. David was nearly incoherent, slurred, utterly deranged with fear. So there I was yet again hopping one more flight, whisking to his rescue, only to find him locked in his flat, starkers, cowering between the bed and wall. I have never felt more sorry for and angry at another human being in my life.

. . . ?

Well, look: it had become perfectly exhausting for me, and I could feel David draining away.

. . . ?

You're tearing me out of myself, I would tell him.

. . . ?

He would just stare at me like I was speaking Romanian.

. . . ?

That was the genuinely unbelievable part. You threw that man on stage and he was one hundred percent fine. He reminded me of those painters with dementia—de Kooning and whatnot. Their muscle memory keeps working long after their brains have left the building. David could run through an entire show faultlessly. Afterward, though—afterward he'd stumble off stage a blithering idiot, unable to put two words together. The drugs had made him unbearable to work with. I realized being in love with him had become like being on fire all the time. We just burned and burned.

. . . ?

No one needed to tell me anything. I was the one who started telling myself: You seriously need to get a life, Angie. This thing you're living? It no longer constitutes one of those.

. . . ?

I knew everything about his story and nothing about mine.

. . . ?

I stopped.

. . . ?

No. I just stopped. I could feel myself doing it. We stayed married, of course, but my love for him—I don't know how to explain it—I could feel it losing its ferocity—those vibrant colors, those incredible notes that had made up the chord of us. Now it was one long, slow fade-out to black.

. . . ?

I could feel my emotions for him cauterizing, is how I would put it.

. . . ?

Oh, well, I'm very good at being dead inside. Everybody tells me so. (Laughs.)

. . . ?

Liberating and devasting.

. . . ?

You pretend someone doesn't matter to you long enough, and eventually he doesn't. Pretense becomes belief.

. . . ?

I won't lie to you. It's always so much easier to be with dumber, less talented, less creatively and intellectually idiosyncratic men. They've all been kinder to me than David. They've traveled less. They've thought less. They've felt less. They are bland as oatmeal and nice as puppies. They are Prozac people, if you know what I mean, even when they're not. The highs and lows are missing from them. The electricity has been shut off for lack of payment. I think people call this being normal. They make perfectly acceptable money. They make perfectly acceptable lives. All they want to do is make me happy. A guy in the military here. A head of pediatrics there. Being with them breaks my heart a few minutes every day. But the rest is thoroughly somewhat bearable.

. . . ?

It just wasn't in me. I told David on day one that I would never divorce him. Maybe it was the last few leaves of Catholicism still floating in my teacup. If he wanted a divorce, I said, he would have to divorce me.

. . . ?

I remember him at some point in his extended stupor looking over at me as we lay together in bed one morning and going: You'll never leave me, Angie Bowie, will you. It was like he'd just figured it out. And I said that's right, David. I'll never leave you, you fucking pud. And I kept my word. I never divorced him. I never even mentioned the word. It never crossed my mind. I was in this whatever you want to call it for the duration.

. . . ?

I couldn't help falling out of love with him for those last six or seven years. More and more I saw people taking advantage of him. I saw him *eroding*, is the word. He wore away. *That's* what really hurt. Yet it snuck up on me I didn't want to be part of it anymore. I *wasn't* part of it anymore, whether I wanted to be or not. The continental drift had become too great.

. . . ?

I raised my head and we were leading altogether separate lives in altogether separate places. He was way over there on one tectonic plate, and I was way over here on another, and we were waving at each other as we got smaller and smaller and smaller.

. . . ?

I kept thinking about how hard I had worked on his career. How he was never going to lift a little finger to help me with mine. It was way too late for that. He'd gotten what he needed out of me. He'd become David Bowie, for fucksake. Several times over. Mind you, I bet if you had asked him back then, he sincerely wouldn't have been able to remember our original promise to each other. It wasn't in him.

. . . ?

David was never one for remembering when forgetting served him better. When it served his purposes, he liked to talk about living in the present. That was his weaponization of Eastern practices so he didn't have to think too hard about his past, take responsibility for what he had done to himself and other people, man up and feel some kind of remorse, accept some kind of guilt, and maybe even learn a thing or two from his own massive self-involved shittiness.

. . . ?

Well, at some point Tony Defries noticed David didn't want me around anymore. Tony knew he couldn't handle me. He knew I could see right through his dude-abides-ness. David was another matter. He invited me to go to Switzerland with him to help him arrange his taxes. I thought sure. Why not? The trip might be a good change of pace. Quieter. Gentler. Maybe we could even somehow find a way back into our re-lationship. Ha. I swear, I'm an incorrigible pillock. It never occurred to me he had asked me there because the divorce laws in Switzerland favored him more than they did in the US or UK.

. . . ?

It was all very cruel. Shortly after we arrived and had settled in he showed up and said: You have to divorce me so we can both be free. Those were his exact words. I looked at him a minute, letting the idea sink in, and said: Okay, fine. There was no more fight left in me. It was time for everything to be over. My gut has never been my friend. I couldn't eat. I couldn't keep things down. I awoke nauseous and had to lie in bed massaging my tummy for hours until I could make a feint at the day. Try as I might, I couldn't stop living all the clichés of a breakup. I knew that's what I was doing. I saw myself doing it. I hated it. I knew I was being an utter fool. But that didn't make any of it easier. There's nothing in the world worse than going from stranger to lover and then back to stranger with someone.

. . . ?

Nineteen-eighty. We divorced in 1980, after living apart for five or six years. There has been complete silence between us ever since. During the proceedings, I told David I wanted only two things from our divorce—a relationship with our son Zowie and enough money to live on until I could establish my own career. I got neither.

. . . ?

Zowie was my present to David. I would never have separated them. Yet I never thought I'd be cut off from my son, never allowed to see him again. On top of that, I was given five hundred thousand pounds to be paid in installments over ten years. That was it. All of David's money I had helped him make, all I had done on his behalf, and that was fucking it. So I was doubly punished when we split. I lost my work, which was David Bowie, and I lost my family, which was Zowie.

. . . ?

He airbrushed me out of his life. You know, like the Soviets used to do with personae non gratae. I heard he had all the photos of us together destroyed. When I tried a few times to call, Coco headed me off and refused to let me speak to him. David was always busy, always out, always something. That's when I heard he began firing anyone who mentioned my name.

. . . ?

No. Seriously. He did.

. . . ?

Famous men often pull that shit when they're threatened by a woman's influence. They like to be thought of as some big one-of-a-kind genius. God forbid any woman helped them get where they were going.

. . . ?

One word: Picasso.

. . . ?

I don't know. Maybe it's that you get to be middle-aged and you're all of a sudden scared and you want to hang out with royalty, so you say it was all a lie and I never meant any of it and you marry a rich, exotic model. The worst thing you can do is become some ridiculous middle-aged boy. I swear to god. Too self-satisfied. Too prosperous. Not able to stand up on your own two feet and say I'm not afraid of losing everything because I think what you're talking about is a load of crap. The Great Rebel in the end wants nothing more than to become a pillar of the establishment. You see it all the time. You want pathetic, I'll show you pathetic.

. . . ?

We didn't know our baby was going to be a boy. We kept ourselves in the dark so we could enjoy the surprise. We chose the name Zowie, you know, because it means life in Greek, rhymes with Bowie, and would fit either gender.

. . . ?

I remember so clearly giving birth in the Bromley Hospital annex. It was painful as hell. But then Zowie came out eight pounds, eight ounces. David was there every second. That was the first and only time I ever saw him cry.

. . . ?

No matter what else, he was a brilliant father. I won't lie. Despite everything, he was devoted and involved. Those early days were so—what's the word? Those early days were so *shimmery*.

. . . ?

David was a late riser. I'd take him his toast and coffee and orange juice in bed when he woke up and run him though his schedule. Sometimes he'd say: No, I think I'm going to the piano for a while. His grand, which was downstairs in Zowie's bedroom—that's where he composed. I remember this one morning he called me in and said: Listen to this. And he started singing *Will you stay in our lovers' story*–you know, the opening to "Kooks." I went and got Zowie and told him: You've got to hear this, darling. Daddy just wrote a song for us. David played it with this huge smile on his face while I danced around the room with our son in my arms.

. . . ?

Why? Today he's a grown man who obviously doesn't want me as his mother. David is dead. I have no intention of reaching out to Zowie again. Duncan. He wants nothing to do with me. Why make myself miserable? I try not to be negative. I have a full and happy life, and I have some fucking awesome memories. That'll have to do.

. . . ?

But there it is, right? You go on. Life lifes all over you. (Laughs.) But enough. Let's talk about something else. Let's talk about my poetry collection.

## HERE COMES THE NIGHT

For the first months after his diagnosis, the man lives as if the news hasn't yet reached him, as if it were still hurtling through otherworldly networks, arcane data entanglements, on its way in.

He continues to grow his next album, bring his musical into being. He phones several local jazz musicians to see if he can get them on board, starts mulling over which recording studio in the area will best serve his needs, reaches out to the New York Theatre Workshop on East 4th to suss out if they might be interested in *Lazarus*.

Strolling toward Caffe Reggio, September morning dank, he is visited by the vision of a young woman with a rat's tail bobbing out from under her dress. She walks toward a dead astronaut—let's call him Major Tom; let's not—lying among dark blue stalagmites on a dark blue planet, eclipsed sun hanging ominously above. Crouching, she lifts the astronaut's visor. His skull is encrusted with jewels. The young woman removes it with the tenderness of a priest laying the host on a congregant's tongue.

The man pulls out of the pedestrian flow, turns onto Minetta Street, excavates his phone, calls Johan Renck, who a couple years ago did that great "Blue Velvet" video for Lana Del Rey.

Picture, the man says without introducing himself when Johan picks up, this—

At first the markings that have commenced appearing inside him, running down sections of his esophagus, look like some sort of runic jabberings, vague and undefined utterances.

The doctors show him what they mean in the X-rays.

They show him what they mean in the MRIs.

The internists prescribe antibiotics and antifungals in an attempt to cover their bases.

While the anomalies don't respond to treatment, they cause the man no discomfort. It is easy to uncouple their presence from his body. They are simply there—unaccountable, persistent, leisurely proliferating, like early winter.

Iman recommends keeping this development from the media. The man agrees. If those bull sharks were to scent his condition, he knows the consequence would be a feeding frenzy that would derail his current undertakings. He therefore leaves careful directions for Coco about how to dodge questions, has his lawyers draw up non-disclosure agreements for the musicians, actors, artists, and friends with whom he is likely to interact, holds back from telling Duncan and Lexi until there is something substantial to tell.

Sometimes when he is writing, a thought from a different sphere strays into him: how every visit to every doctor over the course of your life will advance perfunctorily, except one.

How there will at some point be that look in some physician's eyes, this brief expressive stutter, and then that modulation into a tone of the immoderately gentle, a missionary's feigned kindness.

It is breathtaking to feel from inside out how everything remains as it is this second until all at once it doesn't, because some people will watch TV today and others won't. Some will eat Mexican food, others Indian. Some will get sick and others will never even think of sickness. Some will change tenses while most will remain in the lighthearted present progressive.

This man: he just wants to lead a life.

It isn't a complicated ambition.

He no longer believes being good at things is the point of doing them. He believes doing them jars you in startling ways, makes you a more interesting person. Fans and critics strive to make him more complex than he is. You should see the essays. You should see the monographs. He has always found that amusing. All he really wants to do is put himself in a position where he can't tell if he is making his projects or his projects are making him. There's nothing perplexing about it.

The rest is negligible background radiation, urban sounds you have over the decades attentively forgotten to hear.


He comes upon himself watching a time-lapse sequence condensing weeks of his existence into a short string of optical whiffs. Day becomes night becomes day becomes night as specialists bolt into and out of consultation rooms, technicians ready him for a procedure that has already concluded, Iman zooms up behind him while he works at the kitchen table at two in the morning and throws her arms around his neck and pecks him on the cheek and says *sometimes you will never know the true value of a moment until it becomes a memory* and laughs and disappears from the frame as Coco serial-smokes fourteen cigarettes in five seconds on the sidewalk out back of a hospital and he observes himself in the bathroom mirror lose weight like a deflating balloon and increase his caloric intake and gain a little back again only lose even more as Iman and he begin to consider absconding to their upstate getaway to replenish for a month after they have already returned to Manhattan from doing so and the man grows scruff, shaves it off, grows a mustache, shaves it off, and chord progressions streak onto the pages of his 3.5" x 5.5" Moleskine notebook, skid down faster than he can make sense of, whole new songs arriving in gerbil heartbeats and he is here, in Washington Square, sitting on his favorite bench, the October afternoon cloudless and cool, his back to the Starbucks and Black Box Theatre at NYU across the street, content, still, a *New York Post* he bought on a lark rolled up beside him, itself rolled up inside a Greek newspaper he uses to help him chameleon, nibbling at his chicken sandwich with watercress and tomatoes from Olive's on Prince Street while inspecting the tree branches above him that invent this lucent steam of pineapple-yellow and ketchup-red sunshine.

A woman—close to his age, he would guess, even if from another species—in full-out scare makeup, electrocuted tar-black hair, and a black evening gown tiptoes in high heels behind a Pekingese that looks like a used duster. The man takes pleasure in the realization she doesn't so much as glance in his direction. It makes him feel invisible and cheerful.

Everywhere: children chatter.

Pigeon wings flapping as six or seven birds hop and settle before baby strollers and bicycles, hop and settle.

The light, brisk scent of boiled hotdogs and barbed urine.

He has never learned the names of trees. The man takes a quiet pride in this. He couldn't care less what you call them.

Their names are nothing more than their names. What he cares about is misapprehension. What he cares about is that just because we have this word *leaf* in our vocabulary, everybody believes all the ones on any given tree must be the same leaf. *Leaf* helps people not see leaves. It helps them not see no two are anything except unlike each other.

He swallows a bite of chicken sandwich, unfolds the newspaper within the newspaper across his lap, starts flipping idly, recalling how once Coco took him to a rambling version of *Long Day's Journey into Night.* He slept through so much that he couldn't remember the parts he didn't sleep through. Coco nudged him awake for the curtain call, leaned over and said: Well, that was an expensive nap, boss.

I haven't slept this well since *Parsifal*, the man replied.

Then he stumbles across the photograph of himself back in the gossip section, smiling broadly beside broadly smiling Iman at some fundraiser dinner he can't quite recall having attended, she in her tight faux tiger-skin dress, he in his black tuxedo.

People are saying he doesn't look like himself anymore. They are speculating that he has had work done, or maybe he is losing weight on purpose. Is he developing a new look, preparing for a new role? The man takes out his phone and drops down into the social-media slush. There he learns he may be involved in some sort of cover-up. Is it possible, people inquire, he is part of an obscure conspiracy—although to what end the pundits remain anxiously uncertain? It is a stunt. No. A plea. Groundwork for his next video. Some incredible act of pirate cinema. Some clever, lengthy performance piece that might last years. He has returned to miming. Is readying for a sequel to *Labyrinth*. It is one more placard, the fourth horseman, announcing the arrival of the final battle. Announcing a sour marriage to Iman. They are separated. They have been separated for months. He paid the Mafia to off her. She paid the Mafia to fuck him up. They have never really lived together—that's why there are no photos of the inside of their apartment. They are in marriage counseling. Their marriage is a sham. They have never been happier. It is nothing. A new beginning. A disorderly ending. It isn't him at all, but rather a body double, like the one that replaced Paul McCartney after he was killed in that car crash, like the one that replaced Melania Trump after she chose to leave public life. All you have to do is look. All you have to do is compare the before and after shots to mark the dissimilarities in skeletal structure, the angle at which the jaw sits, the way the face isn't quite right anymore, even if it is tricky to set out why because—because he has gone into hiding, bored of celebrity; become a Howard Hughes, bored of reality; slid back into addiction's mad corrosion: into television, the internet, dominance and submission kink at the ultra-exclusive Snctm sex club. Into ketamine, Adderall, Dexedrine, tanning beds, Botox, eating ashes of the dead, drinking spittle from the living. Maybe he really *is* an alien. Why has no one pointed this out after all these years? What if *The Man Who Fell to Earth* wasn't a fiction after all, but instead a thinly veiled, coded documentary based on Walter Tevis's "novel" that Bowie ghostwrote and published in 1963 by means of time travel? If unimaginably advanced cultures don't have such capabilities, which, pray tell, do? There is surely no evidence to disprove the theory. And what if he has finally been rescued by his brethren, who pulled their planet back from the brink of desiccation by the same means, time travel, and brought him safely home at last? Or maybe he's been an experimental subject for his kind, for the CIA, for the NSA, MI6, Mossad, but never knew it. Or maybe it's something else. Maybe he has finally been netted by the men in black, public interest in his life having waned, and brought to Area 51 for testing. Could it be that he has been enlisted by the Illuminati, the Democrats, the Freemasons, the Deep State, the United Nations, George Soros, the lizard people who control all governments, to bring about global peace once and for all? In any case, Putin is clearly implicated, as is Jeffrey Epstein, Hillary Clinton, and one of Hitler and Eva Braun's sons, Joachim, himself a doddering recluse living deep in the Argentinian rain forest, continuously in search of the fountain of youth. Bill Gates, working in conjunction with the Rockefellers, has always wanted to keep a rock star as a pet in his 66,000-square-foot Xanadu 2.0 estate, as others might an albino python or snow leopard. This much is indisputable. This much is beyond the shadow of a—

The man clicks off his phone, clicks off his optimism about the future of humanity, which he sometimes accidentally stumbles upon himself believing again, and, grinning, wipes his mouth with the handkerchief he keeps in his back pocket, folds up his newspapers, and rises, inhaling a deep lungful of dying leaves and sauteed onions, feeling like one of those morally righteous ecotourists on a ship bound for Antarctica who use biodegradable shampoo and pay through the nose for a two-day front-row seat to the merciless terminus of the world.

The anomalies inch up from his esophagus into his vocal cords, cluttering them with incomprehensibilities.

The oncologists prescribe immunotherapy.

Each week Coco accompanies the man to the outpatient unit, where she reads the latest DeLillo novel and he reclines in a La-Z-Boy for three hours, rock'n'roll cranked up through his earbuds, James Brown, the Fugs, Robert Wyatt, attending the pharmaceuticals coursing through his system, unsure what facial expression he should be exhibiting at times like this.

Afterward, it is as if someone culled his bones. Afterward, he can barely stay awake on the ride home, lies chilled and feverish among jumbles of pillows and quilts on the living room couch, staring in the direction of the television, unable to detect whether the screen is turned on or turned off.

The man occupies the distant end of the spectrum, beyond the audio frequencies that owls and elephants can register.

Sometimes he sits in the panic room for hours on end, listening to Charlie Parker and John Coltrane without being able to hear them, their music evocative now of nothing more than rusty chains and noxious contrails.

He nods off during breakfast, on the toilet at night.

Rashes develop, spread, become itchier by the day, disappear on one area of his body only to resurface on another.

This man who no longer looks fifteen years younger than he is has a mouth that tastes like high school lockers. Every so often he catches himself with his lips parted for no reason, as if he is about to saying something, but has forgotten what.

He spends most of his waking hours dizzy, thoughts boggy and lax.

He wanders from room to room, trying to remember why.

Large furry spiders of colorless hair collect in his brush.

About the time he commits to readjusting in order to figure out how to withstand these new stimuli, eating collapses into a boat rolling on ocean swells. He vomits regularly and spectacularly. The very idea of food spoils into the misshapen and untenable.

Before long he can't even keep down the chicken noodle soup or high-protein smoothies Iman brews up for him.

He can't sleep. He can't stay awake. His joints ache. His gait changes. He looks like he is trying to make his way up the aisle in a moving bus.

His skin thins, bruises.

From a distance his chest appears covered with purple polka dots.

The man is aware his vocabulary is dwindling, that his mind wants to simplify the world beyond repair.

He is aware his sense of specificity is washing out into pastel vagueness.

One rainy Tuesday, bound for the bathroom, he enters a pocket of emptiness and disconnection.


He wakes in Mount Sinai's frantic emergency room, doctors treating him for dehydration and the knot on his forehead.

The man who has never been one hundred percent persuaded he is alive becomes even less so. Everything ensues around him through some thickening diaphanous barrier, in another flat on a different floor—conversations, the solidity of bodies, the clarity and sharpness of scents—as his environment turns into the fugitive awareness of his environment.

Propped upright on the couch, unclear whether it is day or night, the man reaches down to scratch his left calf beneath his robe and discovers with a start that his tattoo has gone kinetic, is flickering violently, swelled into a three-dimensional cartoon, some crazy kaleidoscopic projection.

He fights to bring what he is seeing into understanding. The guy with the frog in his extended palm isn't frozen on the back of the dolphin anymore. He rides it like a Jet Ski, skims through sea spray, bouncing up and down, face wracked with horror, the machine beneath him out of control. The air is no longer comprised of oxygen and nitrogen, but of Niebuhr's prayer, its words strobing, oscillating from *god, grant me the serenity to accept the things I cannot change, courage to change the things I can, and wisdom to know the difference* into *ride the train, I'm far from home, in a season of crime, none need atone.*

All at once the frog bloats into the slick bulk of a hairless bulldog, its eyes red and malevolent.

Bat wings, moist with mucous, unfold across its back.

Before the man can react, the thing catches sight of him, huddles, leaps, welds onto his face.

Recoiling, writhing, the man reaches up to yank it off, unable to inhale, yet somehow it is already merging with his flesh. Its blood is joining his blood, its cells his cells. He can feel those bat wings unfolding wetly from his own shoulder blades.

The translucent lice that make up the thing's breath spill into his lungs.

He tries to scream, call out to Iman—he knows she will be able to help him if he can only get her attention—but his vocal cords are gone.

Terrified, ripping at the thing with both hands, he pushes off the couch and lumbers across the living room in a burst of red butterflies, stumbling over furniture, slamming into door-frames, appalled at the guttural noises fussing out of him.

## LEON TAKES US OUTSIDE

When he opens his eyes again, it is dark, soundless, most windows in the six-story brick building across the street brashly illuminated.

What time is it?

He can't tell.

What day?

He isn't sure.

It is possible five minutes have passed. It is possible five weeks.

His lungs itch.

Somebody has set up a recliner for him beside the waist-high cactus in the living room, from which he can see through mist-drizzle all the way down to the street. Inside one of the bright clothing shops below, a cricket-sized customer in a raincoat shakes out her umbrella. A cricket-sized saleswoman approaches her, gesticulating, her hands tamping the air down before her. Yet the man can see the saleswoman is actually looking over at the door, where somebody else has just stepped in.

He thinks: How nice to call this life home.

He thinks: I wonder where I am.


He closes his eyes to clear his head and opens them again and it is the early years of the nineteenth century. Taken aback, he watches from an oblique angle, some drone shot, as far below the real estate developer the man's blood somehow knows is named John Jacob Astor—as in Astor Place; as in Astoria, Queens; as in the Waldorf-Astoria—glum pinched lips, double chin, wooly eyebrows, shakes hands with a supercilious Frenchman in top hat and tails named Joseph Delacroix, sealing the deal on a lease for forty-five thousand dollars for the swath of the farmland Astor bought a while back.


Except when the man blinks again it isn't that at all, no, it is, what, ten thousand, fifteen thousand years before that handshake, a stubby-legged baby mastodon grazing on tall grass (the man can hear the soggy crunches) in a sunny meadow rolling off into swampland and the turquoise river beyond.


He rubs his temples, this man who no longer looks fifteen years younger than he is, trying to locate himself, come to rest in time, but it is the fifteenth century, he doesn't understand how he knows this, and far beneath him a Lenape boy—his name is Talli—and the boy's girlfriend—Gela—thirteen or fourteen, embrace in secret behind a longhouse at dawn, eyes shut against everything the outside is, tree branches above them forming a lucent steam of pineapple-yellow and ketchup-red sunshine, only—

—only it is 1949, two feet of fresh snow having brought business in the grubby brick warehouses lining Lafayette to a halt. A group of kids has replaced that with their own morning, toppling into a snowball fight in the middle of the street, charging and lobbing and veering and ducking and sliding and falling and rising and charging again. You can make out their laughter. You can make out their shouts all the way up here—

—and the man blinks and meets himself suspended in dirty ice several thousand feet thick, a fly fixed in translucent whiteblue amber, drowning in an absence of sound, taking in the boulders and glacial rubble that hang around him like a mobile of asteroids and space debris—

—while in 2243 it is dead, murky seawater sloshing through the remains of the man's penthouse, windows broken out, roof caved in where the fireplace and easel holding his painting-in-progress used to stand, it occurring fleetingly to him that capitalism always sees the buildings that will eventually oust the ruins, never the ruins that will eventually oust the buildings—

—and Delacroix's resort, Vauxhall Gardens, erupts helter-skelter out of ploughland. Time leaps. Delacroix's lease expires.

There is Astor again, moving in, cutting a new street—a hundred-foot-wide, three-block-long, packed-dirt strip—down the middle of where Delacroix's resort once stood, christening it Lafayette Place in honor of the French aristocrat and military officer who victoriously commanded American troops in the Revolutionary War—

—and Juan Rodriguez, born in the Captaincy General of Santo Domingo to an African mother and Portuguese sailor, known for his remarkable linguistic talents, is hired by the Dutch skipper Thijs Volckenz Mossel, of the Jonge Tobias, to serve as translator on a trading voyage to Mannahattan in 1613. Time leaps. And he has already married into the tribe. Plans flourish. There Rodriquez is, this tiny figure down by the boggy river, first non-native to have settled on the island, erecting his own trading post, thanks to the eighty hatchets, bevy of knives, single musket, and single sword given him by Mossel as the skipper lifts anchor to return—

—while four and a half billion years before that instant a brilliant rotating scarlet and plum cloud of interstellar dust and gas begins contracting in this corner of the galaxy, driven by the shockwave from a nearby supernova—

—only it is Iman turning to look over her shoulder at the fire engines rioting down the street on their way south early one September morning in 2001, chased by the bawling ambulances, and then, for three or four minutes more, lingering on the fashion magazine she is leafing through before the knowledge blows in that it is always good to know things will go on without you—

—except that occurred hundreds of millions of years ago, didn't it, and the view from this oblique angle, this drone shot, has resolved into a terminal beach as far as the man can see, gray sand below a red sun that no longer rises nor sets, a vast dome glowing with dull heat, and some sort of glistening gray creature, a rubbery jellyfish without tentacles, shudders and stills, fighting to advance itself a few centimeters farther toward the smooth lifeless sea—

—and National Guard troops ferry the last inhabitants out of the flooded city in caravan after caravan of high-water vehicles, helicopters, rafts, and hovercrafts at the end of 2124, the infrastructure upon which those inhabitants had depended having gradually miscarried—

—and it is 1967, a squatter-artist named Leslo Nance (late twenties; gold wire-rimmed glasses; ponytail) sinking into a rotten once-maroon couch stenching of mildew, window shards scattered across the warehouse's cement floor, light drizzle misting the early evening outside and in, tries to help a woman named Anne Cellos (late teens; hip-length hair the color of cappuccinos; bellbottoms extending beneath her tie-dyed miniskirt) slumping beside him, work the needle into her arm

—and it is 1643, part of the Director-General of New Netherland Willem Kieft's directive clicking into motion in the same spot the cricket-sized customer with some difficulty folds closed her umbrella: a series of attacks on Lenape camps without approval of the advisory council, against the wishes of the colonists, with the aim of massacring those camps' inhabitants, because, rumor has reached Kieft, the Lenapes are encouraging unification among regional Algonquian tribes against the Dutch—

—and the man and his wife are strolling through the penthouse one June afternoon in 1999 (twenty-six-foot-high ceilings, hunter-green walls, a steal for four million), imagining how they might make it their own were they to go forward with the purchase, pointing to a wall that needs to be blown out here, a kitchen island that needs to be reconstructed there, the man muffling the observation wanting to coalesce in his head that everyone moves through life as a customer now, moves as if owed, hearing himself ask if it might just be possible to have a Jacuzzi for two installed in the bathroom under that window so the couple can attain a nice view of—

—and more buildings flip in to fill the gaps around Astor's marble-fronted, colonnaded mansions, horse-drawn carriages shooting along the thoroughfare, pedestrians dashing in and out among them in the gray haze spewed from those factories this summer day, no, in a snowstorm, a downpour, jerry-rigged boardwalks laid over the mud-slimy, waterlogged boulevard—

—and it isn't that, no, isn't then, but rather a billion years later, a googol—that rawboned single digit trailed by a serpentine tail of a hundred scaly zeroes—when the stars have completed their ebbing out, one after another, until the sky is no longer the sky, temperature no longer temperature, protons no longer protons, time no longer time, and undiluted darkness proliferates through everything that has been known and everything that has been unknown, forever no longer forever—

## RICOCHET

What made you want to read that sentence—if you can call that a sentence?

Seriously?

Let me—do you have a favorite piece of jewelry, Mr. Bowie?

At-home hair-coloring product?

What makes you laugh—I mean really, really laugh?

What's the worst advice you've ever received?

Your views on the most comfy-yet-modish briefs—Calvin Klein? Under Armour Tech 6" Boxerjock?—or are you more a commando man?

Do you ever ask yourself if those around you are continually happier than you, and, if so, why that might be?

What are your thoughts on Manchester United versus, say, Dortmund or Barcelona?

Not exactly the most devout sports fan?

In a perhaps related vein: What makes you want to read yet one more book, when so few have stuck with you over the course of—?

Honestly, though, how many have you actually put down with that intense sensation of having been recreated?

Really?

Doesn't that suggest a rather small benefit-to-risk ratio?

Albums and films ditto?

How frightened were you, when younger, of becoming your parents?

How did that work out?

Did the fear, do you sense, have anything to do with how you swiveled away from relationships lasting more than, say, thirty-five minutes, back in the day?

What profession would you *least* like to belong to?

Wow—I didn't see that one coming—so is there some part of you that believes you could still improve as a musician at this point, and, if so, what would that look like?

Thought experiment: If your phone were to ring as we speak, and you knew, if you were to answer, the voice on the other end of the line would provide you with the definite date, time, cause, and pain scale of your death, would you pick up, or excuse yourself and slip around the corner to Caffe Falai for a custard bombolone, do you think?

Do you imagine that voice as male or female?

What comes to mind, I wonder, when I say *manqué?*

What's the dumbest question you've ever been asked during an interview?

Ah, well, I'll try to do better, then—do you ever climb the stairs to your penthouse, counting, rather than riding the elevator?

I see—does that mean sometimes you get the number of them wrong, thereby beginning to suspect the building may either be contracting or expanding beneath your feet?

At the risk of bluntness—and you obviously should under no conditions answer this if you'd prefer not to—what makes you want to bang out yet another song, another video, at this rather late-ish hour on the life clock?

For real?

Is ageism actually a thing, then, do you think?

Like sexism, only with gravity?

No joke?

I don't—I'm very sorry—but what about that musical you're working on that you know will run only a couple weeks, attaining, all said and done, a sort of footnote status in your body of work—at best?

Couldn't someone argue, as tastemaker Conan Selle did recently in *Revolver*, that aesthetic chances are a tad easier to take when one can afford to recline on the down pillow of one's robust and diversified portfolio?

How does that square with your branding?

How often do you want to google yourself, yet somehow shore up the fortitude to resist?

Have you ever been incapacitated by *reader's* block?

Speaking of which, would you care to remark on the Nat Tate hoax—William Boyd's 1998 faux biography about the imaginary abstract expressionist who destroyed nearly all his output, then leapt to his death from the Staten Island Ferry in 1960?

Yes, but weren't you on the board of the publishing company that brought it out, blurbed the book, and even threw the launch party on April Fool's Day Eve, reading excerpts from Boyd's bio and talking about counterfeit Tate's friendships with both Picasso and Braque—or am I wrong?

Your response, then, to Nacelle Nos's question posed to you periphrastically in, I believe it was, her *Entertainment Weekly* review of said bogus bio: *What varieties of pleasure do you imagine Bowie mined in deliberately deceiving the world in order to benefit financially from his duplicity?*

Forgive me, I didn't mean to—let's—do you find archness relatively easy to deploy against an interviewer who can't defend herself?

No, not at all—I completely understand—I—totally my bad—let's try that again, if you'd be so kind—can you recall the names of your great-grandparents?

Would you be willing to share something now that most people *don't* know about you?

Right, okay, so—no, no, it's quite all right—mum's the word—but I wonder if you could help me out here: what do you suppose your daughter sees in you?

Oh, goodness, no—I don't mean—I'm just—and your son, standing in your overwhelming shadow?

Am I right in my research that you haven't had a number one single in the UK since 1985?

And that would be—let's see—Mick Jagger's and your cover of "Dancing in the Street," correct?

Only the fifth number one UK single in your entire career, if I'm not mistaken?

Would you consider that one of your signature works, Mr. Bowie?

And that tells us—what?

Let me pose what I'm getting at in slightly fresh terms: Is there something that tends to bolt you awake in the middle of what the Swedes call the Hour of the Wolf?

What is your spirit animal?

What's so funny?

Oscar Wilde: *True friends stab you in the front*—first impressions?

Do you ever find it unnerving in the extreme that you know who Justin Bieber is?

Why art?

No, simply that: Why art?

I guess the question behind such a question is this: Does it sometimes amaze you to listen to what you once thought worthy of making?

I—all kidding aside?

What advice would you give these days to the Davy Jones of, oh, 1967—the one who wrote "The Laughing Gnome" in the same year the Beatles did "All You Need Is Love" and the Rolling Stones "Ruby Tuesday"?

Do you define growing up as necessity or calamity?

Are you ever afraid of hanging up your spurs too soon?

Too late?

In 1972 you declared yourself a try-sexual, certifying you'd try anything once—any updates from that front?

Would you agree with Elizabeth I that *The past cannot be cured,* quote unquote?

First thing that pops into your head when I say the words *expiration date?*

Who do you count among your *real* friends these days?

Where do you suppose they've all gone?

Ah, right—let me rephrase: Do you feel you've been genuinely available, emotionally speaking, to anyone over the last, I don't know, thirty years, besides your wife and children?

Well, what I think I'm getting at here is this: Were you by his side when your dad succumbed to pneumonia at fifty-six in 1969?

Were you by your mother's side when she died at eighty-eight in that dog-eared Hertfordshire nursing home?

I've always been curious: Is the story accurate about her once coming upon you covered in makeup after leaving you alone near her vanity for half an hour? Did she actually—as the tale goes—tell you you looked like a clown and shouldn't use it again, and, when you replied *but you do, mummy,* clarify that such matters weren't for little boys, but attractive women and poofters, and you asked, *which am I?* quote unquote?

How many times would you say your mum hit you?

Boy, those were different days, huh?

More than your dad, I would then assume, by a long shot?

I don't see any of the Twilight Saga novels on your reading list—care to comment?

Triumph-over-adversity narrative trajectories, with or without bees, not your cup of tea?

Would you agree with Isabel Allende that men's memoirs are all about answers?

Why are you laughing?

What can you and Iman possibly talk about when you're alone, late at night, in your upstate retreat, only crickets for company?

So the word *love*—?

I see—and when she—?

Nothing beyond what you've already put in print?

Would you take a moment to flesh out the why of that?

On the level?

What would you want left behind when everything else has been taken away?

When you covered "I Got You Babe" with Marianne Faithfull back in 1973, with you all dolled up as Ziggy Stardust and she as a prim nun—how high *were* you?

And that devilish sneer you gave her as you jiggled your furry breasts in her direction—where did *that* come from?

Where has it gone?

Does it ever send a postcard, shoot you a text?

What happened to us, then—you know, all of us, with everything? Can you in a nutshell sketch in that cultural train wreck?

As far as you can tell, were there any survivors?

To switch gears the littlest bit: Your Nazi Period, as people like the theorist Leann Socle now call it—what the heck was *that* about, if I might respectfully ask?

Do you honestly believe any musician, any celebrity whatsoever, could get by with something like that today for more than, I don't know, half a picosecond?

Would you perhaps say a few words about your mother's smile?

What your half-brother's—Terry was his name, yes?—what your half-brother's hug felt like?

What's the first thing that comes to mind when I say: *Me Too?*

Do you reckon your former pubescent groupies would concur?

I'm so sorry, Mr. Bowie, I sincerely didn't mean to—is there something else you would like to—?

Well I suppose what I really want to know is: What is most wonderful about having been sexy once?

No, I don't mean that disrespectfully at *all*—it's just—ageism redux?

How could that conceivably—?

We're not—why are you taking off your mic?

Oh, goodness, now I've done it, haven't I? I didn't mean to—no—categorically not—I vigorously apologize—I suppose at base I'm merely wondering: Do you feel you have a good view of the huddled masses from your Manhattan penthouse?

Mr. Bowie—?

I truly—I've cocked this up horribly, haven't I? I'm a complete novice, as you might—I simply wanted to ask by way of—I'm truly keen to learn: Which gratifications do you find most potent in pretending to be intelligent?

Mr. Bowie—?

Mr. Bowie—?

## ABSOLUTE BEGINNERS

—scribbles Alec Nolens on his canary legal pad in blue ink, confounded it has become mid-November when he wasn't looking, I, we, bird gibber stilled in the courtyard, weather grayed and condemned to a fine rain, the continuous *shhhhhh* of car tires along Prenzlauer Allee roiling up as I step out the front door of the apartment block afternoons on my way to latte and Apfelkuchen with whipped cream (a September surrender), black umbrella bowled above.

Yesterday was mid-June, right? It's remarkable how little one can accomplish if one sets one's mind to it. I understand inspiration is for amateurs. I understand the rest of us just have to turn out with our sleeves rolled up. I understand understanding has nothing to do with anything.

I tailgate the Author's creaky clichés: check out various online news sources to pull a face at reality, post social-media quips to schoolmates I haven't seen in forty years and don't care about in the least except as manifestations of my own nostalgia, visit the Instagram account that not-skinny cat-guy in Maine set up for his potted fern, dive into my first Finnish lesson online at the University of Helsinki, only to recoil from it as if from scalding tap water (*Suomeni on hyvää yötä.* = *My Finnish is goodnight.*), write and rewrite what I wrote and rewrote the day before until the language inadvertently overfluffs, fidgety beneath the overcast worry that what I'll blue-pen next won't even come close to living up to what I blue-penned before, and, so, here we are.

Well, that *and* never wanting this rendering of not-knowing to end. Who wants to conclude a project you care about? That would mean it's done. It's dead. The party's over, the guests gone, the house cluttered with dirty dishes and mum darkness, which means, exactly, what?

Beats me.

That's why I keep bumping into myself forking down speculative slot canyons I know I'll never use in the thing itself. Take

"China Girl," for instance. Co-written with Iggy Pop for his debut solo album, *The Idiot* (1977), rerecorded by Bowie for *Let's Dance* (1983), the latter's single reaching number two for a week in the UK, number ten in the US, while fathering a phenomenal video that beat out Michael Jackson's overcooked "Thriller" at the very first MTV Music Video Awards ceremony in 1984.

Bowie depicts a domino row of female Asian stereotypes (Deadpan Doll, Lotus Blossom Baby, Communist Droid, Hole-in-the-Wall Cook, Mandarin She-Devil, et al.) dominated in various ways (in one scene actually shot in the side of the head, quoting one of the most gruesome images from the Vietnam War: General Loan summarily executing his handcuffed prisoner during the Tet Offensive) by a very white, hypermasculine, nattily dressed (and, oh, my god, what hair—how does he *do* that?) Bowie exuding slick privilege like a prizefighter does perspiration. Some critics beat up the video for racism, sexism, and elitism, which is understandably tempting, given those swastikas dancing in the head of its lyricist:

*My little China girl*
*You shouldn't mess with me*
*I'll ruin everything you are*
*I'll give you television*
*I'll give you eyes of blue*
*I'll give you a man who wants to rule the world*

Except those critics are an aground supertanker, interpretively speaking. Racist? Sexist? Elitist? Only if you're a bad reader.

Only if you have a tin ear for irony.

That makes about as much sense as insights by the likes of Noel Scanel—whose work over the years has satisfyingly met with near-violent indifference—who early on fumbled the interpretive ball by performing criticism as free association, pointing out *China* is shorthand for *China White*—i.e., heroin; *girl* shorthand for *cocaine*; and thus a slam-dunk reveal that the song is in fact about speedballing.

No.

No, it is not.

You think I've been too hard on Bowie at times? You think I've been too easy? Of course I have. I revere him. I'm consumed by him. I therefore have a right to find him lacking. I therefore have a right to find him human.

Here we view a post-seventies incarnation of our superstar, a man who has turned increasingly self-conscious, contemplative, problematically, excitingly political over the years. His *China Girl* jams racism by unconcealing it. Gender-variable Bowie re-presents White Womanizer in order to parody/condemn misogyny and Western orientalization.

From Tiffany Naiman's "Art's Filthy Lesson" in David Bowie: *Critical Perspectives* (New York: Routledge, 2015): *If you ever took Bowie for what was on the surface, you were missing something. I think he was well aware of his elite cosmopolitanism. He was able to move through different cultures because of his privilege but he understood otherness and wanted to highlight that.*

Does Bowie's abbreviated affair with Geeling Ching, the twenty-three year-old New Zealander who played the video's female lead after he plucked her from her waitressing job at a café in Sydney's Chinatown, where most of the footage was shot, help simplify things? Or Ching saying she fell hard for Bowie's intelligence and charm? Or Bowie inviting her to join him on his European tour after the shoot wrapped? Or she accepting enthusiastically and flitting around with him on his private jet, hanging with him in assorted frilly hotels and chichi nightclubs?

Does it help simplify things that in the same year—1983—Bowie cast Aboriginal and white Australians in the "Let's Dance" music video in order to critique racism in Australia? That that was also the year Bowie criticized MTV for its absence of Black musicians? That a *China Girl* in the motion picture industry is a type of test film, an image of a woman accompanied by color bars that appears for a few frames in the reel leader—an emblem of filmic calibration and, in Bowie's visual and linguistic pun, social *re*calibration?

It does not.

Thank goodness.


With our smash-and-dash soi-disant cancel culture, simplified social-media shaming, naïve scrimmage around purported authenticity, subversiveness sure isn't what it used to be.

How pretty to imagine us members of a different, more binary species, where, say, we could all be zipped through a sorting machine and spat out in bow-tied boxes labeled naughty or nice, all ready for Santa. Yes or no. Up or down. Woke or snoozing. Sighted or blind.

The truth, I would like to trumpet here, is really . . .

Only I can't.

How could I?

Is it even possible these days to act like a racist so that one may critique racism? Like a toxic male so that one may castigate toxic masculinity? Like smooth wealth personified so that one may excoriate income inequality?

Fat chance.

And yet.

And yet: Bowie could. Bowie did. In some measure, that's because he has always acted the authentically inauthentic other Other, the ironically queered queer who fell to earth and got trapped in this planet's trappings.

That's why it feels so right watching him play Thomas Newton in Nicolas Roeg's adaptation of Walter Tevis's science fiction novel. An alien who travels to earth to transport water back to his desiccated planet, Newton begets unfathomable revenues on ours by patenting his über-advanced civilization's technologies. Soon he doesn't so much fall in love with as get adopted by Mary-Lou, a (there it is again) mother-substitute hotel employee who, along with a satyric college professor, exposes his mystery's passkey, which leads to the US government capturing him, addicting him to booze, and locking him away in a luxury apartment/dungeon for study.

Although Newton ultimately escapes that local prison, he can't escape the larger one the rest of us live in. He ends up stranded here, alcoholic, devastatingly aware that the family he left behind—perhaps his whole world—has suffered a slow death because of his deficiencies. It's not for nothing that the contact lenses he wears as part of his human disguise become permanently affixed to his eyes when one of the scientists' exams goes wrong.

Newton barely masks his alienness by clothing himself in removable human skin, and yet, even with that skin on, he remains blurrily gendered, emaciated, wobbly on his feet in our estranging gravity, given to femme-fragile nosebleeds and fainting spells.

In other words, Newton radicalizes Bowie's sexual ambiguity: he literally lacks breasts, vagina, or penis, sports bright red androgynous hair reminiscent of another spaceman, Ziggy Stardust, and exhibits an androgynous face and body type. Like Bowie, who never felt fully at home in our terrestrial digs, who was always a stranger to himself and to us, and who had only recently moved from England to America as Roeg began filming, Newton is the congenital outsider possessing a heightened childlike curiosity and detachment concerning his environment and the denizens populating it. That curiosity infatuates and undoes him.

When Dr. Nathan Bryce, said satyric professor, suspects Newton's existential secret, he surreptitiously x-rays him. The result is baffling: a humanoid outline radiating energy, devoid of skeleton or organs—one more blackbox being, all surface encasing interpretive void.

More proof that reading is a mode of laughter in the dark.


In the final scene of *The Man Who Fell to Earth*, you may remember, Bryce hunts down Newton, whom he uncovers sitting drunk, sick, and ageless in his sunglasses and debonair wide-brimmed fedora in a rooftop bar somewhere in the Southwest.

Newton asks Bryce how he tracked him down. Bryce explains: through Newton's coded new album, *The Visitor*. Someday, Newton hopes, if played on the radio, the waves that compose that album, alive with refugee messages, might reach his wife and children—if they haven't already perished long ago at the hands of climate wreck. While the public may think it merely another song, all pop shell without pith, those who get how to listen closely, read acoustically, will hear something quite different.

Nursing his drink, ice cubes chinkling, Newton asks: *Did you like it?*

Bryce: *Not much.*

Newton: *Well, I didn't make it for you, anyway.*

That's when Newton accidentally drops his glass. The waiter rushes over and swoops it up. If the poem formed by the last lines of the film doesn't bruise your rose-colored pipe dreams, I tell my students, then you must push on to learn how to experience art as a full-contact sport:

Waiter: I think maybe Mr. Newton has had enough, don't you?

Bryce: I think maybe he has.

Newton: (chin touching chest in stupor): Ah …

No?

Let me try again. There is another poem, this one by W. S. Merwin in *The Second Four Books of Poems* (Port Townsend, WA: Copper Canyon Press, 1993) that appeared the same year *Black Tie White Noise* did (an album, incidentally, the *Village*

*Voice* gave a B-; *Entertainment Weekly* a D; and *The Rolling Stone Album Guide* a single lonely star out of a possible quintet [*Well, I didn't make it for you, anyway.*]), one year after Bowie married Iman, three before his induction into the Rock and Roll Hall of Fame—there is another poem, this one by W. S. Merwin, whose title is "For the Anniversary of My Death," which opens:

> *Every year without knowing it I have passed the day*
> *When the last fires will wave to me*

Isn't it odd that every twelve months we celebrate the day of our birth, yet let glide by in a hush, unknown and unwanted, the day of our death—though naturally we're all too aware, if we allow ourselves to be, that it's been written down somewhere on the calendar of our lives in invisible ink. Each morning into which we wake could mark the one when our train pulls out of the station for good. Gummed-up arteries. Tobacco's schadenfreude. We are always writing and reading our own elegies. It's simply that we aren't—or, closer to the point, don't want to be—aware that that's what we're doing. Without exception, time's arrow is always speeding toward the center of our disregard.

We are always writing and reading the elegies of those closest to us, too. It's simply that we aren't—u.s.w.

Of the petite, sinewy woman, let's say, hugely more athletic than I—swimmer in high school; rugby player in college; runner in her thirties—always late because she could be, always adorable because she couldn't be anything else, who revered the act of learning almost as much as she did her daily bike race downhill from work at the Geology & Geophysics Department in order to pour our duet of Glenlivets and unwind with me, her spousal hire, on the suburban back deck of our house for half an hour before sampling the dinner I had prepared.

Let's call that woman my wife.

Let's call her my life.

Let's call her Calliope.

Let's say, for argument's sake, that Calli was whooshing down that hill at dusk one mid-November day, a light mizzle suspended in the air, the incurable pothole two feet before the stop sign for an instant apparently misremembered or misinterpreted, the katydid-green Kia at the intersection in the sluggish act of crossing.

Let's say part of love is studiously forgetting to prepare for death.

What I mean to write about are the words *quadriplegia, brain,* and *damage.* How daily I sat by Calli's bedside in the hospital through that primary cataclysm, then through the secondary one that involved not so much her mending as our touching down for keeps on our solitary asteroid, that searing move back home, abundant now with clacking machines and feeding tubes and disposable diapers and soft-spoken caretakers.

What I mean to write about are the sounds that henceforth lifted out of my wife's mouth—if you grasped how to listen closely—how to read acoustically . . . well, you could on a lucky day make out something that approximated a form of maybe-meaning.

Our us was one way.

Our us was another.

And our friends displayed extreme stenciled compassion for the better part of a month, maybe six weeks, and then, having completed their initial obligations, carried on with their own day-to-day whatevers, which I unreservedly understood, while I spent my second sabbatical caring for Calli as much as one insomnious human being can conceivably care for another. I attended a slew of useless support-group meetings where we learned to hurt uselessly together. I attended some gibberish sideshow billed as a spiritual retreat, only couldn't stop myself from giggling five minutes into our first gathering, whose title in the program contained, I kid you not, the words *self-love, plant healing, pranayama*, and *sacred geometry*.

That's how desperate I wasn't.

That's how little I had to offer, to take.

How there is nothing worse you will ever, ever, ever experience than finally, after a forty-minute skirmish, translating what your wife has been trying to express, only to hear it untangle into the shape of a straightforward demand: *Stop ventilator.*


Nothing worse than the limitless panic you will bear, the total war that will ensue between your ears, the last kiss you will bestow upon her cool forehead, until you do what she has begged, what you have to do, what love allows. Nothing worse than the flip of that mint-green switch to off and that first star-tled choke, the unending sound of your wife gagging and heaving herself into reconsideration, pleading with you with her eyes for reprieve, followed by the flip of that mint-green switch to on again.

Nothing worse than when the exact same thing comes to pass three years later—that startled choke, that terrified gagging, that spasmodic heave—except this time neither of you having willed it.

One afternoon it detonates matter-of-factly out of the blue all on its own.

Nothing worse than having to imagine the scene, put its pieces together in your own head after the fact, because you were busy teaching, deep into a conversation with your undergrad seminar called the Postmodern Turn about, absolutely, Bowie's *China Girl* video.

The caretaker was running late.

There was no one around for twenty minutes, thirty max, which wasn't that unusual, you had to get to class on time, and so your wife died alone.

Your wife died alone, and you came to learn it is never the case that you can't locate the appropriate language for what follows. It is rather the case that language can't locate the appropriate language. It isn't as if, if you tried hard enough, you could rummage out the right phrase. It's that our system of communication just can't tolerate certain pressures and torques.

You came to learn—every minute afresh—what Julian Barnes understood since he was thirty-eight: *You don't come out like a train coming out of a tunnel, bursting through the Downs into sunshine and that swift, rattling descent to the Channel; you come out of it as a gull comes out of an oil-slick. You are tarred and feathered for life.*

And, so . . . are we indeed here, on my third sabbatical, my first extended stay away from Calli, immersing myself in the personality of somebody else in order to—u.s.w., inexhaustible?

Do I look up from my work several times an hour, out the window at the stilled courtyard, the grayed weather, the fine December rain suspended, everything shiny and sad, wondering if there comes a moment when piercing loss modulates into perpetual melancholy? Wondering what I should have done sooner, shouldn't have done sooner, could have done other than I did or didn't? Why I cleared out her closet too fast, yet won't take off this thin gold ring, cross my heart, never, no matter what? How godlessness could let something like this lunge into my existence? What Calli might want me to do, how to act, what to think and feel, were she capable of ghosting me one last evening while I was busy scrubbing the grease of the past from my dinner plate? Why our friends entered a cordial, nearly inconspicuous process of shedding me, the condition of perpetual death too much to bear? Why my internist's first reflex was to jot up a hamperful of prescriptions for happy pills, which I immediately collected from the pharmacy, took home, and flushed down the hole in my longing? Why it is that so many women on rainy days look exactly like Calli from behind? That long dark curly hair? That determined forward lean? Why I always have to overtake them, just to make sure, even though I already am? Why I can't summon up the mole on her right shoulder in high definition anymore, her blunt, slightly embarrassing laughter, the touch of her hand reaching for mine in half-sleep? Why it never occurred to me, as I poured our morning coffees, spooned in the sugar, that, if you're in a lifelong relationship, there exists a fifty-fifty chance that you will be the one to lose your partner? Why I sometimes come across myself standing in the cramped bathroom at night, in the black, in all that dead air, asking myself what the end of grief might feel like, how I might be able to recognize it, if it in fact lives in any neighborhood apart from that frequented by self-help manuals, baby-blue tablets, prayerful voodoo, and well-meaning colleagues who haven't a clue, not a clue, and won't until they hear what I'm telling them from the inside out, when they brook the rise and fall of their own quarter? What right creation has to scrawl all over my insides all the time like this? How it is possible to relive in your nightmares, again and again, atrocities you never experienced in waking life, some weird inverse shell shock? How Elizabeth Kübler-Ross could have gotten the works so unbelievably wrong, believing blithely that some beasts can be tamed and contained in a brief laundry list printed in neat block lettering?

*Why don't I feel better yet?*
   *Why don't I feel better yet?*

173

*Why don't I–*
Repeat until the end of the whirled.


## EARTHLINGS ON FIRE

The anomalies fan out through the lining of the man's stomach, overflow into his small intestines, his large.

That's when his doctors begin visiting at night. They show up in his living room, where he sleeps on the couch so he doesn't disturb Iman. Sometimes three of them, sometimes five or six, dressed in baggy black suits like missionaries instead of their daytime white lab coats over summer–sky blue shirts and khakis.

Each is decked in a different style of beard: soul patch, chin curtain, Van Dyke.

Lined up in front of him, hands folded over crotches, they tell him things he can't remember in the morning. He is under the impression they have transcribed the messages developing inside him and come to recite their findings.

Ruin of Flesh, they refer to him as.

While the man is sure—or at least something very close to it—that the doctors' night visits aren't real, that they aren't really standing in front of him at all, what they say seems to make good sense, at least at the time.

We must unceasingly invent people who adore savage gratitude, one of them says, reading from his notes.

Beware the slow rain of charred cats, declaims another.

Nur—, adds a third.

Nur—? repeats the man submerged among pillows and quilts.

I'm working on it, says the doctor in mutton chops. The individual letters are difficult to make out. *N, U, R,* followed by an em dash. Or maybe it's *M, U, R–. M, U, F–* is also conceivable.

German would be one possibility, I should think, says one in a handlebar moustache.


As weeks slur by, the phrases inside the man grow in complexity and legibility. With that, he begins to feel inexplicably better, as though his body might little by little be making a greater sort of sense to itself.

As though he could, if not fully fathom, exactly, then at least intuit the chance of some semblance of knowledge through what is coming to pass albeit not quite wisdom, never that—on the very distant orange-glow skyline.

A fraction of his energy returns.

He learns he can feed himself again, keep down food.

He notices how encouraged Iman seems at the sight of this. Her tentative cheer inspires him to try to improve even more. Over breakfast, he seeps away into her voice as she expresses how proud she is of him.


Before long the doctors curb their rounds. They come by only three nights a week, then only one. Eventually their visits conclude altogether.

Their truancy allows the man to sleep more deeply, serenely, barren of dreams, the thrashing of alligators, than he has slept for the better part of a year.

He moves back into the bedroom, where at nine o'clock every evening he snuggles against his wife, lapses into her pheromones, and closes his eyes.

When he opens them again, everything is pearly winter-morning luminescence.


His stamina accumulates like bubbles collecting in the microscopic cracks on the sides of a glass.


One afternoon, waiting for Iman to return from work, he calls Coco and asks her to let his doctors know the man has decided to stop treatment.

His request streaks up to a satellite and down, his phone overrunning with cell-tower babel.

Then Coco's voice fills every corner of him:

You sure about this, boss?

It's like I've done it before. I realize I haven't, you know, but it feels weirdly familiar, like remembering somebody's name three hours after you tried to but couldn't and all of a sudden, when you think you're not thinking about it anymore, you do.

. . . ?

. . . ?

Everybody loves you, Davy Jones.

. . . ?

. . . ?

I know, the man says. Isn't that remarkable?

Urban dusk. Wet chill. Diesel fumes on the tongue.

A narrow New York street, rush-hour disturbances pressing in, condensing around you.

And it is the man in his sandy-brown cashmere overcoat heading south on foot, crossing Prince, past the five-story mural for Gucci painted across one full side of an apartment building, the bright-cherry garage doors of the fire station, the tenement overrun with parakeet-green fire escapes, the sensation influx, the first time in months he has felt well enough to tackle a walk like this.

Leaning against the wall beneath one of the Corinthian columns outside the Duane Reade at the corner of Lafayette and Spring, a homeless guy in a blimpish navy-blue parka asks him what day it is.

The man stops, reflects.

Wednesday, he says. It's Wednesday.

How do you know? the homeless guy asks, clear and resonant as a professor mid-lecture.

Good question, the man says. I'm not sure.

The homeless guy's hood is pulled up over his head and, despite the atrophying day, he has on dark sunglasses. The only things the man can distinguish about his face are an outburst of glisteny charcoal beard and patches of rosacea.

The man reaches into his pockets for a few dollars.

The homeless guy waves him off.

I'm not married, he says. I don't have a daughter. You don't have to worry. Where you from, bro?

England. I live here now.

Everyone lives here now. What about the rest of your life?

What do you mean?

Your name. What's your name?

Davy.

How do you know? I mean, it's almost Christmas, right? Spam has become especially problematic of late. That's why I teach. That's why the helicopter. You know how come 9/11 happened?

What do you teach? the man asks, taking a place beside him, leaning against the wall beneath the column. He slips his hands into his coat pockets for warmth. For a while, they both attend the pedestrians hurrying past.

The eyes, the homeless guy says. The teeth. Advanced seminars.

Five feet in front of them, a twentysomething woman in a cumbersome doll dress apparently made out of tinfoil meets her twentysomething boyfriend in salmon-pink skinny jeans down to his ankles, yellow socks, olive beanie.

Do I look like a fancy lampshade? she asks him.

They air kiss and move on, keeping a distance that suggests they're strangers.

Walking ashes, the homeless guy says after them, observing the couple blend back into the crowd. Davy isn't much of a name, is it. I'm Josh. I know what the voice box is used for. Hot and cold. Air-conditioning. That's why I teach. The vocal cords are always used straightforward. Which brings us back to 9/11.

Tell me.

Nine-eleven happened so more philosophers could be created. An important nexus in the space-time and so forth. Go forth. No force. Snow fort. Christ is God's selfie. Let me put it another way. You have two girls. Four. Call them sons. Call them pneumatic drills. I didn't know we weren't allowed to love here. If I'd known that, everything would be blue jay. You remember now, don't you: I dropped my cell phone in 2004 and never picked it up again.

Where do you sleep, Josh?

First quantum insurrection on the left. Hey, where the fuck did Monday and Tuesday go? Seriously, man. I mean, you have two girls. Four. I got no enemies. Does the feeling of remorse redeem us? That was the patrol. This is the war. That's the takeaway. That's the takeaway.

I have an idea, the man says. Can I pick us up a couple sandwiches across the street? I've got a bit of an appetite.

What is it? What sort of blueprints? That's the critical. The analytical. The zoophytical. *Religion* is a verb from the Latin, as you may recall, meaning *to wear glasses or spectacles*. *Love* is from the Greek, meaning *to howl or bay*. So you have five rounds or seven. It's up to the clocks, really, if that's the way you want to put it. I was driving my dad's car. This was a long time ago.

What was he like, your dad?

Every policeman is a dentist. You can't *give* everything away. So you have five rounds. You have seven. It's up to you. You can't *give* everything away. It doesn't matter to me. Do you think I can go to England now?

Why?

To see Americans. I'd like to see some Americans. That's where they all live. Sometimes two. Sometimes four. There's a man who buys a suit, buys a hat. You following? He understands, except for the parts he doesn't. That's you, Davy. You have time to answer one more question for me?

Yeah.

This isn't going to stop, is it?

A pudgy bald man in an undershirt opens and leans out the window of a second-floor apartment across the street, smoking a stogie, elbows on ledge, ears twice the size you might expect for a head so small.

Can you wait for me here, Josh? I'll pick up those sandwiches and be back in ten.

That's a Jehovah's Witness yes. Tell me something. Before you go. Do you have any physical evidence for it?

For what?

Today being Wednesday. This troubles me. This troubles the crap out of me. Because at least one molecule of $H_2O$ out of every glass of water you ever drank once passed through a dinosaur. *Bam!* Isn't that the pediatrics? The theatrics beyond orthopedics? At certain income levels, as you may recall, death is unimaginable. From the Sanskrit for *Amazon Devices.* Do you know the Incredible String Band? *The 5000 Spirits of the Layers of the Onion?*

I do.

All life must turn to me. Everybody you've ever fucked, every she, every he, every whatever—just sleazy little tremors in the reptilian complex now, aren't they. These barely discernible lurches in heart rate and body temperature. Am I right? I don't have a hammer. Not for these scapulae. That's the take-away. Everybody has to survive, bro, until they don't.

A bike courier—white skeletal helmet, lime-green shirt, tan canvas messenger bag slung over one shoulder—skims up onto the sidewalk, ricochets among pedestrians, scuds back into the street.

A triceratops of a woman, stooping gingerly to bag her dachshund's shit amid the human river, breaks off singing along to some aria on her iPod, stands erect, and hisses at the courier's receding back.

Walking ashes, Josh says, observing. You got teeth, don't you?

Yeah.

They're mine. You can borrow them. I'm corral with that.

Would you like something to drink, too?

Two girls. Four. So maybe a Coke? Where's the love? It was here a vortex ago. Like God sayeth in Lamentations 3:22: *Don't make me come down there, you dumbfucks.* You're my friend. I like you, dude. That's the patrol. This is the war. The cold-sore centaur.

I like you, too. How long have you been living out here, Josh?

Nine hundred years. It only feels like eight hundred. Things come. Things go. Then they go again. Like family and paper-clips. Only I don't know what a clock is. That's a Jeremiah 29:11. So there's this woman on the outside looking in. Fast: You think she sees me, or is she merely fixing her reflection's hair?

Hard to say, the man answers, patting Josh on the knee. You wait here, okay? I'll be right back.

The man pushes off the wall and steps to the curb, Josh's voice merging with motors and murmurations behind him: Aren't we all just trusting that somebody kept count since the first time Wednesday arrived? When you die, you become science! *When you die, you become science!*

At Chloe's up the block, the man orders two club sandwiches, two sides of fries, six chocolate chip cookies. When he realizes they don't serve Coke, he orders two large mandarin lemonades.

Back at the northeast corner of Lafayette and Spring, he searches for Josh across velocity and commotion. He hasn't moved, is leaning back against the wall, one leg crossed over the other stretched out in front of him, regarding the world as if from a higher plane. The man raises his bags of food and plastic cups above his head until Josh catches sight. He waves with both arms in what strikes the man as a cabalistic version of semaphore, an attempt to communicate directly with all that's growing inside him.

The man waits for the lights to change, crosses among an anxious throng either staring at the asphalt two feet in front of them or glaring humorlessly ahead, daring anyone to enter their holy spheres, talking into hands-free mics as if with demons sharing their skulls.

When the man resurfaces before the Duane Reade, Josh is gone.

The man pivots up and down Spring. He takes a few steps against the rush-hour flow to the corner and scans Lafayette, pushes thirty feet south, backtracks, comes to a standstill in the surge jostling around him.

A big body blunders into his elbow and his lemonades splash across the sidewalk.

Twat, the man says under his breath, and someone beside him answers: Hey, you know where you are, amigo?

The man turns to the source: a Duane Reade security guard, this Hispanic guy of pro-football-sized dimensions dressed in a black knit shirt, black pants, and black Reeboks. The man means to answer something, only immediately forgets what that might be because everywhere around him the first snowflakes of the season are hanging in platinum air, cinders of shine.

I said, the guard says, louder over the clamor, you need some help, amigo? You look a little lost.


## RED SAILS

That night the man tries to summon up his conversation with Josh, jot down in his notebook some of the lines that have remained behind. He wants to fold them into the lyrics on his developing album. A kind of thank you and forgive me.

Next, he tries to summon up Josh himself. Their actual meeting has already begun to turn achromatic. He can picture the Duane Reade. He can picture Josh's blimpish parka. But he can't seem to bring to mind whether or not Josh was wearing gloves, and, if so, what style or color. Can't seem to bring to mind what sort of shoes he might have had on.

Later, back-to-back against Iman in bed, muddying into dreamlessness, the man can no longer locate the homeless guy's name, revive which side of the store they had been leaning against, south or east.

He closes his eyes for a second and then it is the following morning, Coco reminding him over the phone as he repopulates his consciousness that she will be by at nine-thirty to pick him up for his next doctor's appointment.

Something new, they announce in the consultation room: the anomalies have replaced the declarative with the interrogative on the CAT scans. The phrases only spell questions now.

They have continued to metastasize, covering the linings of his remaining organs, creeping into his liver, his brain, his bones.

The man wants to believe something else. He wants to believe in the prospect that he can persist in being the exceptional case he has been his entire life, that biology can function otherwise when it comes to him, even though he knows you are in reality always the passenger on the transatlantic night flight which, from the instant you lean back and tighten your seatbelt at the gate, has already begun to plummet toward the ocean.

All the man has ever wanted, really, when the time came, is an ordinary death. A pain-minimal, barely awake, ordinary death. He knows altogether painless ones are rare, semiconscious ones rarer, but a pain-minimal one seems reasonable to aspire for.

The doctors bunching in the room are using words he once comprehended but can't anymore, not when they are applied to him. They ask if he would like to restart his treatment. He asks what that would accomplish. They use more words he can't quite take in. Coming at him, the syllables are like the quickening at the window that makes you turn, suspecting you either saw a hummingbird or just another floater rising up in your incidental vision.

At the end of the consultation, the man stands and shakes each of his doctors' hands.

Although he appreciates that they do this every day, that several times before noon it is their job to remind patients about the nature of storytelling, the man nonetheless feels the need to thank them for everything they have done on his behalf.

In the doorway, he stops, turns, and a grin breaks across his face.

Have you heard the one about the folk singer, the jazz musician, and the glam rocker? he asks.

Right. So: there's this folksinger, this jazz musician, and this glam rocker. They've been arrested for unspeakable musical delinquencies in a redneck Idaho town and sentenced to death by firing squad on succeeding days. In jail, however, they hatch a plan. Just before each is to be shot, he will shout a warning about some made-up catastrophe at hand. This will distract the hicks with the rifles just long enough for him to slip away. First up is the folksinger. As the police lieutenant counts down from three to zero, the folksinger yells: *Tornado!* The cops reflexively duck, look around anxiously, and scatter. The folksinger darts past them in nothing flat, scrambles up and over the nearby fence, and escapes into the surrounding forest. Next day is the jazz musician's turn. As the lieutenant reaches *two*, the jazz musician screams: *Earthquake!* The cops reflexively drop to the ground, bracing themselves for what's to come, and the jazz musician is history before they can say *Git 'er done*. Last comes the glam rocker. He waits for the lieutenant to reach *one*, biding his time, then hollers: *FIRE!*

## STATION TO STATION

Hey, the man says after dinner, checking out the local evening news while sketching a few video ideas in his notebook. Hey, sweetheart, come look at this.

The man's wife has been soaking in the Jacuzzi after work, listening to vacuous pop music to unbusy her brain, Selena Gomez, Wiz Khalifa, washcloth over eyes, up to her chin in citrus-scented bubble bath.

Iman comes around the corner into the living room in her scarlet kimono decorated with peacocks and white blossoms, hair wrapped in a white towel.

What are we watching? she asks.

The news. We're watching this. He points to the TV, says: Look.

She turns and takes in the screen.

I'm not seeing anything, Davy.

The lead story. They're saying people are showing up in hospitals around the city displaying my symptoms. They're saying CAT scans are showing all these strangenesses inside them.

Where are you seeing this?

I'm seeing this on channel whatever it is. Two. Other people are getting it, is the thing. How is that possible?

His wife steps over and curls in next to him on the couch, legs tucked up under her.

The man does nothing for the next thirty or forty seconds except to occupy her scent.

Lemon soap. Peppermint shampoo. Coconut lotion.

She puts an arm around his shoulders, draws him close. He rests his head on her breasts, falling into fragrances.

You think I'm patient zero? he asks.

But Davy, she says above him.

That I've begun leaking into others?

But Davy.

What if I'm the source?

Davy.

What?

The TV isn't on.

He opens his eyes. The screen is blank, the lights in the living room low, his clicker idle on the coffee table.

Where's my notebook?

I haven't seen it.

When did I turn the TV off?

You didn't, honey. It was like that when I went into the bathroom. It was like that when I came out. You've just been sitting here. What do you say we get you to bed?

I'm scared, he says.

We both are, Davy. Just look at us. What a scared pair of lovers we are. Twenty-three years of scared and counting.


In the antique bench beneath the chiaroscuro painting near the main window at Caffe Reggio, at work daydreaming, the man takes a sip of his espresso and can tell straightaway something isn't right. The nausea washes back in with a vengeance.

He rises with the aim of making it to the bathroom near the counter, only can't even slip from behind the table before pieces of lungs and stomach overgrown with language splosh across the table, across his notebook, coffee cup, plate holding the cannoli.

People nearby lurch back.

The café rattle drops to nonexistent.

The man can't catch his breath. He is choking on his own internal organs. He sticks his fingers in his mouth, back toward his tonsils, extracting wet chunks of himself, clots of musical notes, balled up flesh words. Done, he lifts his head, having forgotten where he is, surveying the appalled faces of the patrons around him, opens his mouth to say something and throws up again.

Done, he dabs his lips with his napkin, and says, looking up at his audience:

Uh, I'm terribly sorry, everybody. I can't—I can't seem to— .

The thought briefly visiting him that, as people move toward the end, they become ever more stunned, numbed, by what they have done and what they haven't done and what is clanging in at them.

He wonders if this is what we have come to call brave.

And next it is this flying, this tumbling faster and faster end over end through minus-454 degrees Fahrenheit and incandescent gas clouds and deep-space gales, those bangs on the nickel-steel-alloy capsule slamming through him, and yet it is also still 1990, he being shown his seat next to his future wife at that dinner party, still turning toward her for the first time and reaching out his hand, even as it is this outrageous racket having stopped, the spinning, and next this noiselessness, he in his beflowered hospital gown sliding slowly out from the giant white MRI cylinder, ass chilly, prick shriveled, the technician in Mylanta-green scrubs and wilted gray pompadour wavering above him, lips moving as he reaches to undo the patient's IV, asking:

How are we doing, Mr. Bowie? Do you think the fentanyl helped a little?

## THRU THESE ARCHITECT'S EYES

A phosphorescent burst, and the man wakes into a recording session, out of breath, head brimming with the sound of himself.

Musty electronics.

Stale cushions.

A microphone dangling before him.

Tony Visconti—thick-rimmed rectangular black glasses, thin close-cropped graywhite hair, faded jean jacket over black T-shirt—gives him a thumbs-up through the foggy pane in the cinnabar-walled control room.

It is the Magic Shop, a five-minute walk south on Crosby. It is 2015.

Wes Craven, mind marshy with slasher clichés and satire, left earth last week. Dylann Roof walked into a Bible-study group at the Emanuel African Methodist Episcopal Church in Charleston two months ago and raised his Glock in a greeting from God. Hundreds of thousands of migrants keep cascading into Europe, suffused with fear and faith.

On *Blackstar*, the man performed all his vocals live with the backing band. He is rerecording them to make sure he has got everything right, curious about the new qualities that enter his voice every day, the surprising tonalities, textures, densities.

He is fairly confident the song he just sang was "Lazarus."

Yes, that's what it was.

He gives a thumbs-up back at Tony, removes his head-phones, joins him at the wrap-around mixing console that reminds him of a steampunk variant of the bridge on the starship Enterprise.

What he has always prized about the Magic Shop is the nondescript gray metal door out front mobbed with graffiti. The small white buzzer come loose on the wall beside it. How easy it is to keep work on an album secret here.

How Lou Reed.

The Ramones.

Blondie, Foo Fighters, Sonic Youth.

In mid-December, he will release this track as a digital download. Twenty-four hours before his birthday and *Blackstar's* release in January, he will upload the video he has started working on with Johan Renck to his Vevo channel on YouTube: frail Bowie in a hospital bed, grayed hair spiky, eyes bandaged, buttons sewn over them, dummy coins to bribe Charon for the crossing to come, sightless yet sighted, then that ludicrously frenetic dance, that scribbling at the desk (*How can you not want to keep living?*) before the final shuffling retreat into the casket-wardrobe from which his cancer—posing as ghoulish dark-haired woman—slunk in the video's opening shot.


Because none of this is rock music anymore. It isn't theater. It hasn't been for decades. How could it? It has become something else. Not that he is quite clear what to call it. Not that it really concerns him

And so what you do is this. You don't use rock musicians to disfigure rock. The problem with rock musicians, especially the young ones, is they want to reinvent the past without knowing anything about it. They want to find their way into comfortable melodies that felt like little sonic riots fifty years ago, become professional forgers when they grow up, the progeny of those currently selling running shoes and toothpaste with the tunes they were once sure would change the world.

There's only one thing worse than young rock musicians, and that's old rock musicians.

And so you recruit a New York jazz quintet led by a consummate local saxophonist, Donny McCaslin, you heard last year down at the 55 Bar in the Village. You dropped in one night because your friend the composer Maria Schneider said that's what you should do and there it was: some rendition of emotive electrojazz you hadn't quite come across before.

Your first reaction was to wonder what you could do with it.

What the man first fell for about Donny was that he could never keep his hair under control. That's unfailingly a good sign. It's like he is perpetually rousing from a long fever dream with a pillow over his head.

And so you email him.

You invite him onto the bus.

Put together and send him demos in preparation for the *Blackstar* sessions. Then step back. Give him room. Become gardener rather than architect.

Let Donny do what he senses he needs to do.

Wait for what comes into view.

The process is like—it's like mixing oils in front of a painting you're on the verge of diving into. It's like not knowing what's going to bud from that first brushstroke on the fresh canvas stretched and tilted before you.

It's that thrill that packs within it alarm and doubt and anticipation and promise, all at once.


Man, Tony says, fooling around with various sliders as the man flumps into the office chair beside him. Your voice is a fucking phantom this afternoon, Davy. Listen to this—

The man looks on while Tony fiddles some more, setting up the playback.

A minute, and Tony adds, mid-tinker: You know this is going to be the most beautiful self-epitaph in the world. You get that, right?

The man takes a photograph of Tony in his head, he loves him so much in this room, in this second.

I'm not done yet, the man says.

He laughs, asks: You think they could tell?

Who?

Donny and the boys.

Not a clue. Everybody kept cursing you behind your back for how much goddamn energy you had. You wouldn't take a break. They hated you for it.

Good. Okay. As long as they hated me. Let's see what we've got.

What we've got is a topple into a looking glass nation where everything sounds unfamiliar—those opening other-dimensional echoes rapidly subsumed by a line of whumping guitar and bass notes, sixty-four human-heartrate beats per minute, only double-time, the drum ticks melting away into woozy A-minor saxophone riffs, the smooth whine of the slide guitar, and that unstable register of Bowie's voice shaded with vibrato, punctuated by a skronky guitar chord from another time zone, and the lyrics sans rhyme, sans chorus, sans shape, this inconsolable expression from some other dimension scorched with that demented sax solo, post-punk dirge sensibility mixed with krautrock's postwar unease translated into the spectrally personal, the impression of someone carried ever farther out to sea, away from framework and decisive coordinates.

After the first listen, Tony strips away the instruments so the man can hear his own voice monopolize the control room, the lonely noise of him straining to catch enough oxygen between lines, the wispy desolation of his lungs.

Maybe Bowie asks him at that point to turn it off.

Maybe he doesn't.

Maybe he wants to learn what annihilation sounds like without accompaniment.

At the hub of Bowie's final transmission is a figure overdetermined with literary associations, adopted by everyone from Melville in *Moby-Dick* and Tennyson in *In Memoriam* to Dostoevsky in *Crime and Punishment*, Eliot in "The Love Song of J. Alfred Prufrock," Sylvia Plath in "Lady Lazarus": one of Christ's most prominent miracles, first narrated in the Gospel of John (11: 1–53)—that sickness, that demise, those four days in the tomb, that resurrection, that inspiration.

Even his name means *God has helped.*

Yet what strikes the reader who listens attentively to the text is that we never actually hear Lazarus's voice. He carries no message himself. John has muzzled him. Christ, too, apparently, who has turned the whole yarn into a sales pitch for himself and his daddums.

Doing so opens an expansive neighborhood for future writers to enter in order to exercise their own interpretive calisthenics. Browning, for instance, in his dramatic mono-logue "An Epistle Containing the Strange Medical Experience of Karshish, the Arab Physician" (1855), tells us Lazarus's de-tour into dying provides him with the present of a child's eyes. He steps from the tomb into a realm that has become virgin-al, everything reimbued with novelty. For him, necrosis is the mother of beauty and awe.

Leonid Nikolaievich Andreyev, playwright, novelist, short-story writer, and father of Russian Expressionism, in 1906 imagines quite a different outcome. Lazarus doesn't discover revelation in cessation. Rather, he discovers nothing except polar cold and modernist darkness. The miracle, he comes to realize, is that there can be no miracle save, perhaps, in the appreciation of obliteration's piercing horror. He steps from his burial chamber with skin rotting, blistering, peeling off, a body bloated and stinking, a face frozen in shock before what he has witnessed, a mind already putrefying around the edges. His interest in his life, let alone the hereafter, has desert-ed him. For Andreyev's Lazarus, forced return is bottomless trauma. He abhors his newly acquired knowledge that his life has been a living death.

Eugene O'Neill's *Lazarus Laughed* (1925) presents us with a series of episodes in which Lazarus's faith is tested in various ways upon his reappearance. Members of his family are taken from him. His wife is poisoned. And in the last scene Lazarus himself is gagged and set on fire at the stake. Even as his flesh bubbles, chars, and flakes away in black shreds, his eyes shine forth with comprehension. The emperor Tiberius orders the gag removed so that he can give Lazarus one last chance to answer the frantic questions he has been posing all along: *Why are we born? What waits for us beyond?*

This time Lazarus chooses to reply.

*Eternity*, he says. *Stars and dust. God's eternal laughter.*

In other words, the book of Job written by Camus, which is to say the answer is, without exception, ever another question.

Each retelling provides us, not with some kind of epiphany—perish the gullible thought—but rather with the articulation of the human struggle to articulate the human struggle to articulate.


The central allusion behind the image of the black star which guides the album's argument is, cf. above, to that slang term for the radial lesion on mammograms announcing breast cancer.

Behind it, however, lurks an auxiliary one, this to a rare song by Elvis Presley, with whom, you will remember, Bowie shared his January 8 birthday.

In 1960 Presley recorded a jangly country-western called "Black Star" for a Donald Siegel film by the same name in which he portrays the son of an Indian and a white settler. (N.b. Andy Warhol's famous silk screen diptych of Elvis the cowboy was plucked from this flick three years later.) In the song, we learn we all have a black star loitering over our shoulder. To catch sight of it is to know our time has come. The speaker therefore refuses to look behind him as he rides, demands the black star stay back there where it belongs, for he still has plenty of living to get on with, lots of dreams to make come true.

The film's title, though, was eventually changed to *Flaming Star*. The studio ditched Presley's original song and had him record a revamped version to reflect that change. The initial "Black Star" recording blipped off the radar until 1991, when it was released on *Collector's Gold*, the Elvis boxed set.

Bowie both references its thematics and gives Presley and himself a mortal birthday boon.

Most misreadings of Bowie's song reside in the mistaken belief that Bowie casts himself as Lazarus. He doesn't. Listeners tend to glom on to that first line—*Look up here, I'm in heaven*—to argue the piece's speaker is already dead. But he isn't. He's simply so potted on painkillers—*I'm so high it makes my brain whirl*—that it kind of feels that way. The rest of the lyrics are all about, not holidaying in kingdom come, but the speaker's physical and mental unlacing, his fright in the face of reaching room temperature, his useless appetite for release, his glance back over his life, and his recognition that your prominence and portfolio diversification count for lots less than nil once you're close to joining Mother Nature's ultimate democratic party.

After learning Lazarus is ill, Jesus peddles his snake oil to the window-shoppers dawdling around him: *This sickness will not end in death. No. It is for God's glory so that God's Son may be glorified through it. He who believes in me will live, even though he dies.*

But Bowie himself doesn't live.

That's not the point.

He shakes hands with Elvis.

He's not Lazarus.

His music is.

## JUMP THEY SAY

The nightly news shows a glossy black SUV pulling up to the New York Theatre Workshop for the musical's opening. The predictable herding. The hoots. The raised cell phones. The camera flashes a glitter of insults.

The car door swings open and the bodyguards spill out around the couple, Iman leading the way, the man trailing six or seven steps behind.

The nightly news shows the man's gray hair having overtaken his sandy brown, cut close like an accountant's, stubble-length sides, the antithesis of anyone's idea of stylish.

You can catch a hipster in the background saying to a friend, as if to convince himself: *That's him all right.*

An older woman calling: *Love you! Woo-hoo!*

It is December seventh.

It is a Monday.

The temperature edging up near fifty despite the hour and season.

It is forty years since Thomas Newton was abandoned on that rooftop bar by Dr. Bryce somewhere in the southwest, bereft, rich, alcoholic, ageless. Nowadays he lives in a stripped-down

New York penthouse, an alternate-reality Bowie in some out-landish time warp, unable to die, unable to live, subsisting on gin and Twinkies and memory itches about where he isn't any-more, his lost family, his maternal lover Mary-Lou. Over the one hundred twenty minutes without intermission Elly, Newton's recently hired personal assistant, transfigures into her, picking up Mary-Lou's looks and mannerisms, softening into love with Newton despite her age, his, despite her marriage to somebody else, despite the others around him still exploiting the man who fell to earth, promising him even at this late date a return to the stars—despite the indications sprouting that none of what we are witnessing is real or ever has been: that these people, that even we the audience, are simply so many fictional characters who have unintentionally stumbled into a three-dimensional televi-sion set whose channels won't stop flipping inside Newton's head, switching pitch and genre until, in the last scene, we encoun-ter him sprawled on the floor, maybe dead, maybe mad, maybe somehow having slipped away only to rise again some other day in some other place . . . although this last reading, the musical's title notwithstanding, is for reckless optimists only.

Notice for a moment, all the same, how much the nightly news misses.

It neglects to show, by way of illustration, the rubble the man's immune system has become.

It neglects to point out the thirty-four days left inside him.

Only fifteen seconds long, the footage of his arrival at the New York Theatre Workshop moves too fast to follow in any detail.

You have to slow it down, blow up each instant on your screen, before you can begin to see what is going on.

Look—there: how forced the man's smile is.

Closer: how his teeth protrude negligibly as his sick gums recede.

He isn't wearing makeup any longer. His pasty skin appears almost translucent in patches.

Look at the pallid green vein near his left temple, the age spots on his left cheek.

Look at his neck.

Remark how slender it has become.

Look at his ears.

Remark how large they have grown.

See his skinny legs.

His wide feminine hips.

How he carries his head inappreciably forward this evening, reminiscent of a professor in his seventies.

How his gait is off, a scarcely noticeable lumber having invaded it.

Who is he?

Who is this man?

This is the man moving across a brief stretch of opening night, yet for him that brief stretch is boundless and radiant with adoration, fascination, those flashes, that continuous cell phone scintillation.

What is this man thinking?

He is thinking every step is a battle.

Observe how he avoids meeting the eyes of his fans.

How he bores down on the entrance to the theater, closing the gap between him and it as quickly as possible.

And what is the saddest sight in these fifteen seconds?

There: how painstakingly he clutches a small bottle of water to his stomach with both hands, like it might slip out of his grip and into another reality if he isn't careful as the bodyguards barrel him through the covey of onlookers—many fewer than he may have expected: not hundreds, not scores, but, playing the footage over and over, you count, at most, thirty.

Why does this man move like that?

This man moves like that because he is beelining backstage, shedding his environment as he goes.

What does this man want more than anything when he gets there?

To collapse into a chair, any chair, sapped, shot, exhausted by his hundred-foot slog.

He wants a few minutes to collect himself before the curtains go up and he is required to appear interested in others again, shrug on his David Bowie, that suit of lead.

In light of this, look at the footage once more.

Take your time.

Look at those fistful of seconds decelerated, enlarged.

Now: Who is he? Who is this man?

What can you determine he is not forgetting, repeatedly?

You can determine he is not forgetting, repeatedly, that the future will fail to include him.

He is imagining every territory he will not inhabit, all the people, the books, the crucial objects that will burn to the ground.

What else does the nightly news omit?

The nightly news omits what occurs when our plots slow down, when those mechanisms that drive them—combat, acclaim, evasion, promise, pain—lose their urgency, their scope, diffuse into the lives we all in truth occupy, if steadily less and less.

The nightly news does not show that the only thing separating one human being from another is, ruthlessly, the architecture of the body.

It does not show that wintry Sundays for the man as a boy were roast lamb, mashed potatoes and peas, the fire blazing in the living room, his mother, father, half-brother, and him listening to *Two Way Family Favourites* on the wireless, his mother singing along to the record requests and, afterward, the broadcast signing off, taking a shrill moment to remind his father that she could have been a singer, a star, even, had it not been for everything he was.

His father's ensuing silence at these Sunday congregations, how he had been organized since childhood to duck strife, dodge anger, no matter the cost.

The nightly news does not show Terry cringing on the rose carpet by the fireside whenever his mother lashed out like that, hard, cold, isolate, how he was conscientiously learning to live deeper inside himself with each ambush.

It does not show how easy it is to love another human being so long as you don't know them very well.

Without exception: the greater the abstraction, the greater the ability to love.

It does not show Alec Nolens, him, me, comprehending with a mild shock how despondent a freshly tidied third-floor apartment in a leafy, cobblestoned neighborhood of Berlin can look when three suitcases stand at attention inside the front door, five boxes of books and index cards piled beside them, ready to taxi to the post office on the way to the airport.

The nightly news does not show the man quietly stopping his treatment for cancer less than a month before his musical opened, or how in his early fifties he visited a funeral home, picked out an unadorned coffin, and asked to lie in it for an hour in a vacant room, to take in that exceptional class of silence.

Or how in late December he emailed his friend Gary Oldman to elucidate his impending disappearance, concluding his note: *That's the bad news. The good is I've got my cheekbones back.*

It does not show Duncan Bowie, weighing in at eight pounds, eight ounces, first taking the stage in Bromley Hospital on May 30, 1971, his birth so ferocious that after thirty hours it cracked Angie's pelvis, while her husband lounged at home listening to Neil Young records.

It does not show the man's father asphyxiating alone in an upstairs room, trying to get to the oxygen tank just out of his reach, because his mother chose to nurse her husband herself, but from a distant part of their house, where she didn't have to listen to his struggle.

That the only thing making some days tolerable for the man was intolerable uncertainty, because intolerable uncertainty proved to him tomorrow could perhaps be other than today.

That the man was so strapped for cash in his early twenties he was forced to take a job operating the photocopier at Legastat, having over the course of a handful of months miscarried auditions for *The Virgin Soldiers, Alain,* and *Oh What a Lovely War,* Decca having rejected three of his songs for single release, Apple his album, BBC his latest play, everyone agreeing he displayed a modicum of innate talent, but nothing special, nothing in any way worth pursuing.

The nightly news does not show Alec Nolens, him, me, standing inside said apartment door, staring at those suit-cases and boxes, waiting for the cab, wondering what this year has amounted to beyond another sheaf of muddled pages.

It does not show the evening in 1978 when the man tentatively brought up the idea of divorce with Angie for the first time, she responded by popping one bottle of sleeping pills and another of tranquilizers while sloshing in a warm lilac-scented bubble bath, and the paramedics accidentally dropped her semicon-scious body down the staircase on their jumble to the ambu-lance, thereby fracturing her nose.

The suspicion springing to mind in his coked-out rapture that his parents might prove to have been robots all along—if not that, then *why?*

The man coming to terms with the notion that what counts in life is how nimbly you can walk through flames every second you are awake.

It does not show the evening Tony Visconti and he stood stoned and obsessed with UFOs on the top-floor balcony of a red-faced Irish friend's flat in West Hampstead, the friend de-claring after a long lull *They're up there all the time,* and pointing, and the man raising his head to spot a rapidly moving pin-point of light. *It's just a satellite,* Tony said. *Keep watching,* said the friend. With that, the pinpoint performed a ninety-degree turn, sped up, and evaporated into the night sky. Or so the man would remember it decades later.

His father returning from work with a stack of that new dwarfed variety of record called 45s, and how the boy, nine, crouched over the family turntable after dinner, twirling it faster and faster to get the thing to play them at the right speed, listening to contorted versions of the Moonglows, the Platters, Fats Domino . . . and then the silvery bewilderment of Little Richard banging out "Tutti Frutti," the living room instantly congested with hard-driving energy and berserk lyrics and bright colors and flagrant provocation, life from one pulse to the next becoming anything can happen.

Nor the boy, convinced he had just heard remarks from God, decamping the following day in search of a photograph of the deity himself, discovering in the pages of a music magazine down at the local record shop Little Richard's garish Black flamboyance, his unsettling makeup, his androgynous bouffant, the first eyeliner and lip gloss of glam rock exciting in the boy's crotch a dozen years before the fact.

It does not show him, me, Alec Nolens hauling each box, then each suitcase, down three flights of stairs and out onto the street, the neighbors he passes—growling old guy with scabious skin beneath graywhite beard bristle; teen girl in a black fedora earbudded into her life's soundtrack—hugging the wall to avoid meeting his eyes.

The recognition and celebration that everything, positively everything, lives between quotation marks.

It does not show the man meeting absurdist master mimes Lindsay Kemp (beefy, bald, a mouth full of hissy s's, the quintessential queen) and his boyfriend Orlando (petite, legally blind, virtually silent, matching pate), touring their bazaar of bizarre, learning mime from afar, dance from up close, and initiating an affair with the former that would take up the first chunk of each evening back then, only for the man to sneak over to Kemp's designer Natasha Korniloff's flat afterward to round out his randy.

Instead, it shows a reviewer talking about the musical, the film on which it was based, its songs, its actors, its stage set, its extraterrestrial angst.

It shows a reviewer talking about the man's expedition into the empire of alter egos that has stretched over nearly five decades, how he manufactured a vigorous career based on being there while never being there.

The nightly news does not show me, him, et alia locking the apartment door for the last time, slipping the key in the mailbox, and stepping into shimmery spring sunshine and concentrated scent of green, taxi waiting, trunk hood raised like an amazed mouth.

It does not show how we live in a world always at the brink of giving in.

How we are nonetheless arranged to refuse conclusion.

Or how the man for a few years when he was young came to agree with what Charles Bukowski (cf. the reference to his poem "Bluebird" in the last stanza of "Lazarus") was supposed to have written in a letter, yet, it turns out, did not: *You should find what you love, and let it kill you.*

And how that changed.

And how that kept changing.

And how Iman, upon their return home from the opening that Monday evening, will need to help her husband undress.

Help him urinate.

Help wipe up the spatters on the floor around the toilet.

The nightly news does not describe how touching the man's skin feels to his wife—is it warm, cool, soft, parched, busy with too many reminders?—nor what runs through her thoughts as she does so.

The nightly news does not record what crosses her mind when she kisses him goodnight and recalls that nowadays he tastes of decay.

The nightly news does not describe the scent of the couple's sheets, the firmness of their mattress, whether tonight the man will sleep there or, out of kindness for her, out of an appreciation for his wife's need for hush, among the pillows and quilts on the mattress in the sensory-deprivation tank of the panic room, listening to the high-pitched whine of his own nerves firing.

It does not show the dream the man will chance upon with the help of a sedative: both his lungs all at once beginning to glow in his chest, through his ribs and flesh, blurry balls of light, as he stands by the cactus at the window, and how that light swiftly expands to engulf him, and then the living room, and then the city, and then the universe.

What the man will make of that dream when it wakes him inside the hour of the wolf.

How, lying there, mulling it over, the man will hope one day to understand it.

The nightly news does not show what he feels as these reflections traverse his synapses at two hundred seventy miles per hour.

What is the man experiencing?

What he is experiencing now?

And now?

The nightly news does not show the man experiencing a kind
of love story, experiencing this:

## 5:15 THE ANGELS HAVE GONE

Let me tell you a love story, Iman says, leaning back in a sleek
black Swedish chair by his hospital bed set up in the panic
room, a Glenlivet over ice cupped in her hands, feet on black
footstool. Let me tell you the kind in which there isn't one. You
shouldn't feel bad. This story is just the town most people find
themselves living in sooner or later.
    You expect one place.
    You get another.
    Endlessly.

My parents also started out in love. Theirs was what their friends
described as a grand romance. My mother was fourteen when
her parents arranged her marriage with an older man in Mogadishu. Shortly before the wedding, however, she fell in love with
somebody else—a handsome Arabic teacher from Ethiopia.

He was seventeen.

He was kind and funny and smart and passionate and perfect.

And so they eloped, much to their parents' exasperation.

The newlyweds colonized their own country by populating it with two boys and two girls. In 1955 they brought me to join them. They named me *Zahara*. In Arabic it means both *flowering* and *shining*. You know this already. You know it was a name that condemned me to being a woman. My parents sent me to live with my grandparents, and after that to boarding school in Egypt, because they still had too much they wanted to accomplish before pretending to grow up.

But my grandfather—he couldn't tolerate the idea of me dragging a woman's name behind me through the years, and so he renamed me *Iman*.

I tell people I was the only girl in Somalia who grew up within a man's name.


You already know these things, babe.

I know you already know these things.

But I need to tell them to you anyway.

I need to know you're listening.


My mother and father didn't fall out of love in one stroke. It's almost never like that. The process was more gradual, involved.

They simply—how does one say it?—they simply sunk into the ordinary a few more inches every day. We understand how this is. The heat of passion and romance thaw into some lukewarm pedestrianism. Wild lovemaking melts into *Did you wash my shirt, did you get the leaky faucet fixed, did you remember to pick up the humus on your way home?*

The excitement of the engagement ring becomes the ring of the telephone announcing the latest chore necessary to keep the industry of marriage humming along evenly from one week to the next.

It's discouraging to know how many things are true in the world.

Like you, I didn't love my mother. I don't understand why hearing that upsets some people. Why would we necessarily love someone just because we echo a few strands of their DNA?

She was stubborn. I was stubborn. She imagined herself an independent woman. I imagined myself an independent woman. She followed her whims. I followed my whims. She was a gynecologist, and gynecologists see women as a series of likely errors, body parts with blunders waiting to break out.

How could we possibly have gotten along?

Like you, I was much closer to my father. I was about to say he became a diplomat, the Somali ambassador to Saudi Arabia. However, the truth is he didn't *become* one. He was *born* one. It was in his blood. He intuited how to coax others into feeling like they could work together. He had the ability to gently show adversaries that it is better to solve difficulties instead of perpetuating them.

You could hear his beliefs in the tone of his sentences and see them in his compassionate eyes.

I spent most of my childhood and adolescence away from home, hating every mile that separated me from my family. I was certain when I was away that they stopped loving me. Yet, when I returned on holiday, I remember how my father acted as if no time at all had passed since I had last been there. I remember how much he prized reading to me before I went to sleep each night. It didn't matter how old I was, whether I was five or fifteen. It didn't matter how tired he was. My father would sit next to my bed, as I am sitting next to yours, and act out all the characters, put on a different voice for each.

How he made me laugh.

Even today, whenever I pick up a book, I see him in its pages. Whenever I read, I hear my father reading it to me in my heart.

Abdirashid Ali Sharmarke, our president, was shot dead by one of his bodyguards in 1969.

The day after he was lowered into the ground a coup d'état stormed across our land, and every truth in Somalia canted overnight.

Within two days, my country failed.

The virtuous became evil.

The evil became virtuous.

Everyone who represented the old guard, my father included, became an enemy of the state.

My family was forced to flee by foot into Kenya.

This sounds more dramatic than it was. You know one simply does what one has to in order to get what one wants. It was the same for you, in a manner of speaking, wasn't it. How strange to learn what two people can have in common.

I have never understood those who vacuous along in life—letting happen, as they say, what will happen.

Those people make excuses, say everything occurs for a reason.

They say what's meant to be is what's meant to be.

Those people are full in equal measures of gullibility and horseshit.

They must be among the saddest and most bitter people on earth.

My family was forced to flee by foot into Kenya. So what? We all are forced to flee our home at some point in our adolescence if we have decided to be alive enough. And so that's what we did.

For a few months in Nairobi, I studied political science at the university. To support myself, I worked as a waitress and translator.

You know this part of the story.

You know how one morning on my way to class in my favorite bright yellow sari I stopped to window-shop at a couple boutiques downtown when Peter approached me and asked if I had ever been photographed.

I was incensed.

I stood there in the middle of the sidewalk, shouting at him to fuck off, convinced he was just another fucking white man who assumes we savages live in mud huts and believe cameras steal your souls.

Peter was terribly embarrassed for us both.

Passersby stopped and gawked.

He politely endured my virtuous wrath in the polluted urban heat, then explained he was a professional photographer who would like to take a few shots of me to show around New York.

He was struck, he said, by what a born model I was.

I didn't trust him, despite his good looks and manners.

I said sure, but his photos would cost him eight thousand US—the price, I was figuring, of my college tuition.

He didn't miss a beat.

That sounds fair, he said.

He said: Let's get going.


Peter Beard always kept his word. He took what turned out to be nearly six hundred photos. *Six hundred.* A week later, he called me from New York and asked if I would join him there.

He introduced me to the people at the biggest agency in Manhattan, Wilhelmina. They hired me immediately. My first job proved to be with Arthur Elgort. He was photographing me for *Vogue*. You've seen the pictures. It was madness. Here I was this college girl walking down a street in Nairobi's city center in my favorite bright yellow sari. Here I was making ten thousand dollars a day in New York by doing nothing more than waiting in front of a lens. All I had done was go window-shopping on my way to class.

Only then I looked at what Arthur had done. Oh my god. The same thing used to happen to you all the time, didn't it. I was stunned. I couldn't recognize myself in any of his pictures.

Who was this woman? Where did she come from and why was she making believe she was me? There was no trace of Iman in her. She was nothing except surfaces and fancy jewelry and shiny skin.

This is modeling?

This is what Americans call beauty?

From that moment on, I wanted out.

Not a month had gone by, and already I had come to realize modeling was a horrible profession. You know this. I know this. Ghastly. Just ghastly. You've heard me do nothing but complain.

I hated everything about it.

Except the money.

The money I adored.

It wasn't long before I was making thirty thousand dollars a day.

How can you not fall in love with thirty thousand dollars a day?

It was prostitution without the sex. Without the physical sex. It was prostitution without touch. Your currency is your image.

Yet tell me: how was this living?

My parents were heartbroken. My father had wanted me to go into politics. He had wanted me to follow in his footsteps. That was my plan. Only now every time I spoke with my mother and him on the phone, they asked me when I was going to get a proper job.

The newspapers started calling me the Black Cinderella.

I thought: Fine. Okay. Fuck you all. You use me. I use you. In the long run, we'll both get what we need.

I know you know this.

But I want to hear you listening.

I want to hear you really listening for a change.

Davy?

You know this and you know about the man named Hassan Gedi who came forward in the media, claiming I was his wife, claiming we had lived together for two and a half years back in Kenya and that he still loved me and wanted me to return.

He was telling the truth.

That's the part that hurt.

We had married when I was eighteen, despite the fact—maybe because of it—that my parents were dead set against it.

Gedi was an entrepreneur and Hilton hotel executive. He made a good living. My parents said I was too young. They told me I only thought I was in love. Give it time and the feeling would wear off.

I reminded them how old they were when they got married.

I couldn't have said it better, my father told me with his compassionate eyes.

I do everything I can to avoid admitting I am wrong. It is not in my nature. You know this about me. But I was wrong. Marrying Gedi had been a terrible mistake. He was a bully and I was a stupid child. I leapt first, then I looked, and now I had to pay for it.

I had left him three months after our wedding. We didn't get a legal divorce because I had divorced him in my mind. I flicked a switch and stopped feeling him, stopped thinking about him, stopped caring about him. One day he was my husband. The next he was nothing. I shoved him and his nice suits and Armani cologne out of my memory.

Only there he was again, reborn.

The paparazzi couldn't get enough.

Some people maintain that they hold no regrets about what their younger selves did. They maintain life is all about moving forward and never looking back. These people are dimwits in the morning, imbeciles in the afternoon, and morons in the evening.

You and I both know the past is nothing except a calendar of regrets.

If somebody hasn't grasped that about living, he hasn't grasped a thing.

I was sure my backstory with Gedi coming to light would destroy my career. Instead, I discovered this was Manhattan. In Manhattan, nobody cares what you do. In Manhattan, there are no morals, only money, only images, only the stock market of your reputation in the gossip columns.

My job was to sell illusion, so my publicist and I sold it.

We worked hard to maintain my public aura of innocence, kindheartedness, and elegant beauty.

Behind the scenes, I divorced Gedi—legally this time— while promising myself I would never marry again.

Why would anyone want to knowingly become someone else's twice in one's lifetime?

I loved my grandfather very much.

Do you know what he used to tell me?

He used to tell me: *Don't set out on a journey using someone else's donkey.*

He used to say: *You don't go searching for bones in a lion's den.*

I believed my grandfather with all my heart—until I met Spencer.

Excuse me for laughing.

You had a splendid, svelte, girlish body, babe. How I adored exploring it. But Spencer's—Spencer's body was a mountain.

I know you don't want to hear this, but I need to tell you anyway.

Are you listening, Davy?

I need to know somewhere deep in your morphine visions you can somehow hear this before you leave me.

Spencer was playing for the Knicks. A mutual friend set up a blind lunch date for us in a nice Soho bistro and accompanied us to make sure everything remained seemly.

Afterward, Spencer escorted my friend and me back to his apartment. I was floored. It was filled with an extensive collection of African art. I would never have thought the jock

I talked to over lunch about basketball and running shoes was capable of such things.

As he walked around showing us this piece and that, sharing his knowledge of my continent's cultures and histories, I could feel myself falling for the surprise of him.

Most Americans assume Africans live in trees, believe in forest spirits, and carry a special wisdom within them. Spencer knew far more about my continent than I did. I was so impressed. Within days we began jogging together and taking strolls through Central Park. He would hold my hand like we were in high school, just like you used to do. He opened doors for me and walked on the street side of the sidewalk. Whenever he met me, he was holding a little gift in his hands.

I could feel the power I had over him swelling. It felt marvelous. There's nothing in the world like gaining power over a man.

I faithfully learned about basketball and attended almost all his games.

We had a—we had a good time together.

Not great, mind you, but good.

Very good.

Five months after our first date, I found myself pregnant. Spencer may have turned out to be many things. Back then, though, he was honorable. He proposed at once. In part, of course, this was because of the baby. But in part it was also because he knew our marriage would get me my green card, something I needed to remain in the States, and he wanted to help me any way he could.

And that's how Zulekha—her name means *brilliant beau-ty*—how I delight in the sounds of it—arrived in this world.

For nearly a decade Spencer and I were—how to say it?—we were happy enough. We were, in any event, a long way into that condition termed *married*.

Yet almost straightaway the happy-enough commenced falling to pieces.

The moment *Vogue* and *Playboy* approached me about posing nude, Spencer and I began quarreling. He didn't want me to get my breasts enlarged. He didn't want me to show my naked body to anyone else. He told me this was beneath me. I told him it was a measured fiscal decision.

We argued all the time.

I was keenly aware I had to make as much money as I could as quickly as I could. Every day models feel time eating away at them—just like you rock'n'rollers. Obsolescence lay on the other side of the next photo shoot. I had already crested thirty. My body knew it didn't have many shoots left in it. I had to work hard as long as my looks hung on.

Spencer wouldn't hear of it.

I went ahead anyway.

Naturally I did.

Why would I care what my husband thinks?

Shortly before he was traded to the Lakers, and we moved out to LA, he started snorting cocaine. It hurt so much to see that. He got tangled up in the glamor contraption. As his habit worsened, his game suffered. He fell into that series of clichés.

You know the ones I mean.

It wasn't long before he was wandering around in a perpetual coke-haze—that feeling you will live forever and the world is out to get you any second.

In the beginning I tried not to notice, but everything got out of hand. I finally confronted him. I told him he had to stop or I would divorce him. I shouted. He shouted. And then out of nowhere he hit me. He *hit* me. Not hard, mind you—a cupped hand on the ear—but it didn't matter: in that instant we were over.

I phoned the police and had him arrested.

During our divorce proceedings, I found out he had fathered a child by another woman while we were still married.

That tore me to bits, but it also allowed me to win custody of Zulekha.

And, like a shot, there I was, all at once thirty-four. I had two bad marriages behind me. I had a child. And the only thing I wanted was to put a close to the lunacy, draw up a new map.

So I retired from modeling. I moved back to Manhattan. I started looking around for what to do next.

And there you were.


Are you listening, Davy?

It's—let me see—it's five in the morning.

You have to keep listening just a little longer.

I know it's difficult, but this is where you think you know what's coming, only you don't have a clue.

Let me just freshen up my Scotch—

. . .

.  .  .


.  .  .


So my hairdresser, Teddy Antolin, threw a big birthday party for himself. It was October 14, 1990. Remember? Of course you do. I was chatting with someone to my left—I can't bring to mind who—when I heard somebody else being seated to my right.

I turned and—

It still feels awkward admitting how little I knew about you. Just that you were this big star. Along with everybody else on the planet, I had listened to a few of your hits when I was growing up. They had left almost no impression on me. There was "Changes." There was—what was it called?—"Young Americans." I very much liked that one, how it takes down a backward country that thinks it's better than it is.

And, needless to say, for a while there was "Space Oddity" playing on every radio station you turned to, which, to be honest, I didn't particularly care for.

Otherwise, nothing.

You took my hand like a gentleman. I could tell right away you were acting. It didn't matter. Then you took your seat and started talking. Nonstop. I could tell you thought you were proving to me how smart you were, how cultivated.

You showed off like peacocks do.

You embarrassed yourself.

Truth to tell, I can't remember what you said. Isn't that funny? I'm sure you were deeply taken with yourself, but all I remember is wishing you would stop mansplaining the universe. I wanted nothing more than to enjoy my dinner in peace.

It was all quite annoying, really.

Still, the party eventually wound down.

You took my hand once more, told me how good it was to meet me, and left.

I thought: How would you know whether or not it was good to meet me? You didn't let me get in a word edgewise.

Next day I flew out to LA on some business and you dropped away.


Yet who was waiting for me in the terminal when I returned, this bouquet of flowers clutched to his chest among a horde of fans?

You stood there with that fantastic smile you wore when you needed something.

From that day on, you wouldn't stop courting me.

It was plain enough you thought I was falling for you. Remember how we were walking through Greenwich Village that time and you noticed one of my sneakers was untied? How right there you got down on your knees and retied it for me in front of all the passersby?

Or, later, how on that trip to Florence I saw a ring I fell in love with in the shop window? You filed away the happiness on my face and, when you were ready to propose, secretly flew back to Florence to buy it, only to discover it had been sold. You and Coco tracked down the owner and made her an offer far beyond the ring's actual worth.

You read me very well.

You were terrifically sweet and refined.

I knew this was all one of your masks, but I let us follow the script you wrote for us to see where it would lead.

You flew me to Paris and rented a boat on the Seine. It became apparent to me you wanted us to live in a Hugh Grant movie. After dinner, the city lights shimmering on the water around us, you asked me to marry you.

Suffice it to say it was October 14 again.

What a detail man you were.

The pianist played "April in Paris"—the same song you played for me yourself at our wedding.

Which is to say the movie you had us occupy was insanely saccharine.

It was adorable and pitiful seeing how vulnerable you were, watching you believe you were in love with me simply because you pretended to be in love with me so long you came to buy into your own performance.

Still, it felt good to give you the kind of smile I had never seen you wear before.

It felt—

. . .


. . .


. . .


Remember how it took us a while to fully find the words for the fact that you—we—hadn't wanted a marriage so much as a merger?

We wanted an effective partnership, I guess you could say.

I hope hearing that doesn't upset you.

I'm trying very hard to be as honest as I can be.

What I'm doing isn't—

. . .

. . .

. . .

. . .

. . .

I wonder if it's fair to say about humans that what we really love to do is to hurt each other in all kinds of ways. What we really love to do is to open each other's unhealable wounds time and again to see what will happen.

Except we can't admit such a thing, can we.

Society will never allow candor like that.

We want to believe in a reality other than the one we see around us, so instead we spend our lives trying to disguise what we are doing to each other by using different words for it.

We learn to call harm love.

We learn to call being injured empathy.

There was never any doubt in my mind that we were fond of each other. Don't misunderstand me. We enjoyed each other's company immensely. I know that. You know that. We could talk for hours about anything.

If we had been the same sex, babe, we would have been best friends.

Only we weren't the same sex.

We were both excellent businesspeople and we appreciated that we needed a specific brand for this phase of our careers. We needed to become the archetypal beautiful, high-profile, lucrative, happy couple.

And so that's what we became.

Granted: I don't recollect us ever actually putting it that way, do you? I'm not sure we had the emotional firepower for that. Rather, we just enacted the concept every day, strumming the media with the same ease with which you strummed your guitar.

. . .

. . .

. . .

That reminds me.

You know I was never especially interested in your music. I think you already appreciate that. I would attend one of your concerts every once in a while for the benefit of the paparazzi, but you could tell most of your work bored me.

Tin Machine?

That electronica fluff with Eno?

And traveling with you wouldn't have made sense, given my own schedule. I had too much I wanted to achieve. I told you as kindly as I could. Speaking in a mother-voice colored with a few white lies sometimes got through to you. Only

227

mostly you would will yourself not to take in what I said behind what I said.

You had this extraordinary capacity to go deaf when it served your purposes.

You were a hearing impairment with a cute grin.

You couldn't have cared less about my intention to start up a cosmetics company for women of color. I didn't blame you. How could I? Who in the world can get excited about a strategic move like that?

You wished me well.

I wished you well.

You dutifully did what I asked you to do.

You helped me by letting us be seen together, and I did the same for you.

We both recognized this basic principle: Keep the media well-fed, and our capital would take care of itself.


Here is more you don't want to hear: You are eight years older than I am. You've been ill off and on for more than a decade.

I don't mean to cause you pain, Davy, not now, not ever. I sincerely mean that. Yet you have to understand in some essential way that I didn't need you.

That I found you ever less appealing.

Once in a while, I caught myself wondering if you had ever really been up for the challenge of us.

To a certain extent, I'm sure, you wanted to be my big brother from the outset. You wanted to be my father and protector. I get that. But tell me: Why do you think I would have wanted such a thing, and how do you think that ever could have lasted?

You busied yourself in your provinces.

I busied myself in mine.

Period.

. . .

. . .

. . .

. . .

. . .

For the most part I went along with the script you had written for us because, I imagine, I didn't have to take care of you the way most wives have to take care of their husbands. I was too selfish. Plus you had Coco and her team to supply your needs. Even now you have your round-the-clock nurses.

You haven't had to do a thing for yourself since you were fifteen.

It occurs to me maybe that's why it took us seven years before we seriously tried for a baby. What do you think? You had at last begun to tour less, had more time to donate to getting fathering right.

The thought of that became important for you.

Little by little, it felt right to bring Lexi into our lives.

Do you remember how magnificent the day she was born was?

You were by my side in the delivery room. You cut the umbilical cord. I could feel you there at fifty-three, fully concentrated into those hours, cherishing the sensations associated with becoming a real dad for the first time in your life.

We may not have gotten many days right together, but that one we nailed perfectly.

Not that you were a great parent.

You know that.

You know you were adequate at best.

We liked to sell you to the media as this fabulous dad, only you and I both were aware that wasn't the case. You refused to change Lexi's diapers. You wouldn't get up in the middle of the night to tend her. And god forbid Lexi or I bothered you while you were working.

It wasn't just about her, was it.

It was about me, too, the way you pitched into yourself for days on end.

You astounded me by how thoroughly you could shut off your connection with us, how easily you could switch off your emotions and distance everyone around you.

You made passive aggression into high art.

When in doubt, you took refuge behind that ridiculous version of Buddhism you mobilized when it happened to suit you—you know, desire is the root of all suffering and blah, blah, blah.

Good god, babe. Really?

You think it wasn't the easiest thing in the world to see through you?

You think we missed it—how you stopped talking, how we faded into wallpaper beings, this background noise that, once it's been in the room with you for a while, is awfully easy to overlook?

And you had the nerve to tell *me* I pushed *you* away?

Tell me about deciding to tour again on behalf of the *Reality* album. Tell me about 2003. Tell me you honestly believed I didn't know what you were up to when you were on the road, didn't think I had people who would report to me about your gorgeous young Japanese and Black boys and your aging women groupies.

You were the master at keeping the half-secret.

. . .


. . .


. . .

Tell me deep down you didn't want me to know.

Tell me about all the people you would never be there for.

Go on.

Try.

. . .


. . .


. . .


. . .

. . .

I thought a lot about leaving you. Of course I did. I know it's
hard to explain. Only—only I came to cherish you and hate
you together, just like most couples do.

You were my joy.

You were my misery.

Somewhere in there something broke between us. We
crashed so many times, yet you never seemed to notice. Did
Coco ever tell you I started calling you Mr. Oblivious behind
your back? It felt much better than it should have.

Somewhere in there it came to feel like we had never had
a chance in the first place.

Sometimes I wanted to stop what we were doing and ask:
Did you ever really love me, even for a little while?

I got good at putting on a smile for you without being able to
figure out what to say or do next. You know what I mean? At
some point we could no longer locate what we were looking for
in each other's eyes.

It regularly crossed my mind I should take what I could and
walk out the door with Lexi—and then you ended up writing
songs about it without acknowledging that's what you were
doing, even to yourself.

I'm not sure I can put into words exactly why I stayed, except
to say I guess you know I never wanted anyone more than I
wanted you.

How can I say that after saying everything else?

. . .

. . .

. . .

I don't know.

. . .

. . .

. . .

It has something to do, I suppose, with the prison house of history we constructed for ourselves. With the unrealistic story I told myself a long time ago about what Lexi's childhood should look like. With how we lie to ourselves, and those gossip columnists, and looking sixty and feeling sixty and being sixty, and the fact that I knew you better than any other person I would ever know in my life.

It also has something to do with how sorry I felt for you.

When I got that call from Germany about your heart attack, it was so odd. Before the doctor on the other end of the line had finished, I knew I wasn't going to quit us before you did.

It wasn't in me.

. . .

. . .

. . .

And so here we are, babe.

You're leaving me.

That's where we—

I'm going to call in Duncan and Lexi and Coco now so they can say their goodbyes, too.

. . .

. . .

. . .

. . .

. . .

Wait. Before I do, I want you to hear something else. I want you to hear me say I don't love you. Not anymore. Don't get me wrong, Davy. I did. I'm sure of it.
   I'm almost sure I did.

. . .

. . .


. . .


Are you there?


Davy?


Looking back, I can see that feeling has been gone for ages.

You stopped earning it. You became an ailing old man turned into yourself, masquerading as some sort of sage.

Why did you do that to us?

Why did you turn off my favorite movie?

I know.

I know.

I know.

Let me get the others.


Let me kiss your cheek first—

That's nice.

I'll always miss you, Davy Jones.

You know that, right?

I've missed you so much over the years.

## YOUR TURN TO DRIVE

Let me tell you a love story, Iman says, leaning back in a sleek black Swedish chair by his hospital bed set up next to what used to be their king-size one in what used to be the room they shared, curled into each other.

Let me tell you the kind, she says, hand resting protectively on her neck, in which there is a love story inside a love story inside a love story.

That's how I picture us when I close my eyes.

We both expected to wind up living someplace else.

Yet somehow we found ourselves living among all these tendernesses.


You remember how I told you I was chatting with someone on my left at Teddy Antolin's birthday party—I can't recall who—it didn't matter—it doesn't matter—because when I heard somebody else being seated on my right I turned, and there you were.

You took my hand. I was startled by how soft and feminine it was. I noticed you'd even got a manicure for the evening.

And, Davy, that smile you gave me—

I found everything about you immediately, intolerably sexy.

Our chemicals made us fall for each other on the spot.

All we had to do was follow them.

There I was, convinced until that minute I never wanted to get involved with anyone again—especially someone like you. I had had enough big stars and spoiled rich boys. I was fed up with the business of business and the glamor of glamor. I was fed up with everything about the reformatory I had been trapped in.

Only tell me this: how could I help myself?

Have you seen that Davy Jones guy?

Oh my goodness.

He raided me with comfort—this fierce and abiding sense of comfort—this split-second realization that you have known somebody all your life, even though you are meeting for the first time.

I sat there listening to you trying to impress me. You went on about how you were currently being blown away by Faulkner's *As I Lay Dying*. I remember this so well. You described the Museum of Jurassic Technology and how you always stopped by when you were in Los Angeles to unearth ideas.

You talked about how you considered the avant-garde a kind of dress-up box that you liked rummaging through as if it were your mother's closet.

I couldn't stop listening.

I couldn't stop looking.

I couldn't stop thinking how adorable you were.

I kept telling myself how fortunate we were to have met each other at this time in our lives.

It felt like stepping off a plane in a new country. The texture of the air. The smells. The preposterous language the people around you are speaking.

Everything unusual.

Everything brand new.

You already know this, Davy.

    I know you already know this.

    But I need to tell you anyway.

    I need to know even deep in your morphine visions you can somehow hear me.

Are you listening?

Are you there?

I need to know you remember how Teddy's party wound down before we knew it. You took my hand again, told me how good it was to meet me, and left because I told you I had to fly out to LA on business the next day.

    When I exited the Jetway upon my return, I saw all these people clustered around someone famous, snapping photos.

    The crowd thinned and I saw it was you.

    You were holding a bouquet of flowers in your hands, waiting to welcome me back to New York.

    You should have seen my heart grow right there.

. . .

. . .

. . .

I know—I know from the outside, without fail, love stories sound like strings of banalities.

From the inside it isn't like that at all.

From the inside they form long hallways of astonishments.

I feel so sorry for people who have never dared to open that door and enter.

. . .

. . .

. . .

I'm not as good with words as you are.

I can't ever quite say what I mean.

It's—

. . .

. . .

. . .

Sometimes I think language amounts to less than whispers in a storm.

I know you know what I mean, even if I can't say it right.

You tell it backward for the media for effect, only you know as well as I do that I proposed to you first.

Remember the Italian dinner I cooked over at my place?

I spent hours preparing it.

The candles?

Bach in the background?

How we were both so amazed we were never at a loss for words or laughter? We could have talked for weeks on end and, done, would have felt as if we had simply got ready to begin.

That's who we are.

Do you know what I'm saying?

Who thought best friends could find each other so far into their lives?

I need you to remember I told you that evening how taken I was by your inquisitiveness, the way you had worked out over the years how to become someone other than the person you had been when you were young.

That's an enormously difficult task.

Most people are too frightened even to begin to contemplate a voyage as precarious as that one. They want nothing more than for tomorrow to be the same as yesterday, only securer, warmer and snugger, while making believe they have somehow grown a few inches in the direction of wisdom.

. . .

. . .

. . .

Remember I told you how I treasured all the lives we had lived before we met, how neither of us would have given up a single one of them, I was sure, yet how I appreciated far more that those lives were behind us?

I need you to remember I told you how taken I was by how much you knew, how you were always tuning in to new music and films and plays, by the way you read to me lying on my couch—do you remember?—both of us naked, your legs draped over mine, my head on your chest, savoring the rush of your breath through your heartbeat, you reciting passages from the book that had most excited you that week.

It was like being a little girl again.

It was like swimming in a cloud of glitter.

I would close my eyes when we were like that, just receiving the vibrations flowing from far inside your ribcage.

I could live inside the scent of your skin forever.

I told you how lush—that's the word I used, remember?—how lush it had been being with you, how you had already exposed me to more than I could ever have been on my own, how I couldn't wait to see what you would introduce me to next.

Every day I was with you, I learned something I hadn't known before I woke up.

I told you how taken I was by your feminine qualities, just as you had been by my masculine ones, the way we reveled in exploring them, each other, the way our cells became so ecstatic celebrating our us-ness.

After dinner I brought out two glasses of champagne, a little bowl of chocolate-covered almonds, and the little gift-wrapped box I had prepared.

Inside was your engagement ring.

I'm flying through air right now, Davy Jones, I said. Quick. Marry me.

If you can't hear anything else I'm telling you, sweetheart, hear that.

It's the only thing that matters.

Quick.

Marry me.

. . .

. . .

. . .

. . .

. . .

We turned into the kind of couple who resembled an advertisement for a kind of couple.

We made all our time together look like a first date.

It shocked us as much as it did others.

Given who we had been, where the pop-psychologist gamblers had placed their bets, what were our chances?

I don't know how, exactly, but we created a way to teach each other it was time to stop being images and start being humans. We helped each other formulate the choreography for our love. We could never stop asking each other questions because we always wanted to learn more about each other. We promised ourselves we would never go to bed angry. If we caught ourselves bickering, we invoked the law we made early on saying we would have to pay each other the fine of one nickel. How could anyone bicker seriously after paying a nickel's fine?

. . .

. . .

. . .

You know how I loved my grandfather very much?

He used to tell me: *To be without a friend is poverty.*

He used to say: *If two people come together, they can even mend a crack in the sky.*

No matter how many years you and I spent together, it was never enough. No matter what came to pass in our lives, we knew there was one other person out there we could always turn to, rely on, confide in—somebody who would always care about us, try to feel what we were feeling, provide us with a home beyond home no matter what continent our bodies happened to be on at the moment.

We were like little knowing children, and it was beautiful.

Can you hear me, Davy?
    It's almost five in the morning.
    It's Sunday.
    Your birthday was two days ago.
    You're sixty-nine now.
    How can that be?
    Since then the hours have all slurred together. It doesn't feel like we're anywhere. It doesn't feel like it's any time.

. . .

. . .

. . .

I know you have to leave soon.
    I can hear it in your breathing.
    Only—

. . .

. . .

Do you have any idea how much I loved cooking for you? It gave me such pleasure. It was like holding you in a different way.
    Do you remember how every Sunday I made us a fried breakfast so you could get a regular taste of England? Sausages, eggs, baked beans, tomatoes and mushrooms, toast, coffee.
    What a good time I had trying out new recipes.

Do you remember how, on the fourteenth of every month, you sent me flowers to remind us of ourselves?

I thought surely you would eventually begin forgetting, except you never did.


It was funny, wasn't it—how we saw ourselves wanting to go out less. Who needs to socialize? we said. That just means you haven't found real companionship yet. We became increasingly bored by topics addressed for the sake of maintaining a tranquilizing social drone.

We remarked how fewer of our friends were connected to the business. Moby lived nearby. Tony Oursler. Annie Leibovitz. But mostly we hung out with people as far from our professional duties as possible. The farther away, the better.

Every three or four weeks we threw a dinner party for some of them, and afterward gathered in the living room for a screening of whatever documentary or film or series had caught our eye recently.

Remember how we couldn't stop laughing as we watched all thirteen episodes of *Extras*?

Ricky Gervais's sting.

His flagrantly awkward, stupid, self-defeating characters.

Those insults coupled with self-deprecation, provocation, and excruciatingly uncomfortable scenes about topics no one is supposed to talk about these days in that tone?

Oh my goodness.

*That's me!*, you kept saying to everybody. *If you x-rayed them, that's what ALL English people look like inside.*

Others used to tell us how lucky we were, as if it were a criticism.

How lucky and how privileged.

You could hear all the shades of envy and resentment rustling through their voices.

Only you caught them off-guard with your response, couched in one of your sweet grins: *Don't forget incredibly bright and driven and talented, too,* you'd say. *We shouldn't leave those out of the equation, should we?*

We wanted to make sure we were really where we wanted to be before we got serious about trying for a baby.

Who would have thought it would take us seven years?

You came to the decision to tour less. You said you'd like to wander away from your music for a while and just be a parent. You told me how happy John Lennon had been with Sean and Yoko those years he dropped out of public view.

I powered back my own schedule to accommodate this new city we decided to build.

Do you remember how magnificent the day Lexi was born was?

Seven pounds, four ounces.

Those old-soul brown eyes opening upon this world.

You were by my side in the delivery room. You cut the umbilical cord. I could feel you there, all of fifty-three years old, fully concentrated into the sensations, cherishing the process of becoming a dad.

Thank you for those hours, Davy.

There were so many days we got right, sweetheart, but that one goes down as one of the best.

. . .


. . .


. . .

Do you have any idea how much it meant to me seeing you get up every morning before Lexi so you could be the first to welcome her into her day?

How much it meant seeing you read to her, just like you read to me?

How we would all get down on the floor and play together for a whole afternoon, the rest of the pressures tumbling away?

It was all about the three of us.

Shamelessly, joyously so.

It was so comical watching you, Mr. Aladdin Sane, Mr. Ziggy Stardust, changing into the measured, sensible, relaxed father-as-mother while I solidified into the mother-as-father.

Who could have—


Do you remember that man and his little boy you met by the slides on the Houston Street playground with Lexi?

I forget their names. All I recall is how your paths began to cross every weekend, how Lexi and his little boy played together, how you only talked music with him once or twice in passing. Mostly it was the kids, pleasant empty chitchat, maybe a few observations about today's traffic or weather.

Remember how you told me his first words to you were: *I didn't think I'd ever see you in a park?*

You were so hurt you came home straightaway to tell me.

Why do you think he could imagine I wouldn't take my own daughter out to play? you asked.

You seriously couldn't fathom it.

After all these years, *that's* who Davy Jones has turned into.

. . .


. . .


. . .


Together we were great at ducking the paparazzi, weren't we, until it dawned on us the paparazzi didn't really care that much about us anymore.

Not in Manhattan.

Not at this stage in our lives.

They had younger, hipper, more exciting quarries to stalk.

We got to slip into the exquisite cliché of a mom-and-dad routine—early morning school runs and soccer games and music classes and the sweetness of watching you steadily evolve into even more of a homebody than me.

I loved you so much for that.

Remember how I still sometimes wanted to go out to parties back then? How you declined nearly every invitation you got? How, at the door, as I was about to leave, you would give me a little kiss and tell me to have a good time?

It took a while before I could get my mind around why you didn't want to come with me, and then it hit me: there was nothing you hadn't already seen and done.

You had attended all the parties there had ever been.

There was never going to be a reason to attend another.

I don't need any more attention, you used to say. I've absorbed all the attention I can take. You only need that shite when you're incapable of connecting with another person in any meaningful way.

I don't have any more temptations, you said.

Zero.

Then added: Well, coffee, maybe.

When you decided to go back on the road, I attended as many of your concerts as I could. It was hard with work, and I'm sorry I missed as many as I did, but it was so nice to be there, watching you dazzle everybody. It made me proud, like I was up there with you on the stage.

I get why people aren't supposed to feel this way at our age, except I don't care: when you were on the road, and I wasn't with you, it was physically painful for me. I'd be lost. On the outside it appeared as if I was merely going about my daily business. Inside I'd be waiting for your next phone call or text. They were little bright bursts of light in my day. There I'd be, hurrying down some street to a meeting, and all of a sudden I wouldn't know where I was or where I was going.

How splendid that was, Davy, these memos from the universe saying we were still us.

And when you came home, remember how we always held a little party for ourselves? I wore your favorite lingerie—from our first night together.


I know your whole body, every mole, every blemish, like the back of my own hand.

How I loved kissing every millimeter of you.

Sometimes you would send me a text the next day that would simply read: *mmmmmmmmmmm.*

. . .


. . .


. . .

I never told you this, but sometimes I dreamed I was part of your body.

Could you guess?

In the dream, we had become inseparable.


Some days I wish I could go back in life—not to change anything—not at all—just to feel a few things twice.

. . .

. . .

. . .

Can you tell it's dawn, Davy?

Light is creeping in everywhere.

. . .

. . .

. . .

Are you still there?

I wish I—

. . .

. . .

. . .

When you go away, it will be unimaginably difficult to describe to others how sad I am.

How sad I will be every minute for the rest of my life, even when I am laughing with somebody else or giving Lexi a hug.

It will be another one of those whispers in the storm.

You will always be in every one of my cells.
      You know this.
      You've always known this.
      That's why I will never be lonely.

. . .


. . .


. . .

Can you tell I'm crying, Davy?

Can you hear it in my voice?

It's like our memories are slipping down my cheeks.

. . .


. . .


. . .

Look at us.

Look at where we ended up.

Here in this room.

. . .

. . .

. . .

We've been married almost a quarter of a century.
How can you leave somebody after all that time?
It's impossible.
Think about where we came from.
Think about where we landed.
I don't understand any of it.

. . .

. . .

. . .

Is it almost time, sweetheart?

I can sense you going away.

Should I call in Lexi, Duncan, and Coco?

. . .

. . .

. . .

I want you to hear me promise you something first.
I want you to hear me promise you I will never remarry.

What a mad idea. You can't take apart one story without re-placing it with another, and I will never take apart ours.

I promise you will never be my late husband, Davy Jones.

I promise you will always be the man I love.

. . .

. . .

. . .

Thank you for letting me live in our favorite movie.

. . .

. . .

. . .

Okay—let me get the others—but let me kiss your cheek once more before I—

That's nice.

That's so nice, my love.

. . .

. . .

. . .

I'll always miss you, Davy Jones.

　　You know that, right?

I will miss you and miss you and miss you and miss you and
miss you.

## ALWAYS CRASHING IN THE SAME CAR (I)

The nightly news shows a heavily bespectacled Gary Oldman
taking the stage at the BRIT Awards on February 24, 2016,
six and a half weeks after Bowie's death, to earnest applause
and the intro to "The Next Day," in the video for which Oldman plays that horny priest in a brothel the Catholic Church
condemned.

　　Oldman stands in an ocean of blueberry and ruby light
reminiscent of Las Vegas casinos, here to accept the statue for
his friend's outstanding lifetime contribution to music.

Take a close look at the footage.

　　It's easy to find on YouTube.

　　Go ahead.

Closer.

Seriously.

I am very near certain you will agree that Oldman acutely believes the words he is reciting during the four-minute-and-thirty-nine-second acceptance speech, which mostly praises how Bowie faced his cancer with humor, courage, and grace; extols Bowie's musical originality, experimentation, and exploration.

Yet that doesn't prevent you from also noting that Oldman is obviously acting, hamming it up with his quietly tragic theatrical voice, overdoing it with the emotions in order to help his audience feel what they are supposed to feel, sweep them up in the evening's splash and ratings.

In other words, he is doing what he does for a living because he has found himself in front of a large group of people wanting to encounter heartache and devotion, enlightenment and good value.

Toward the end, however, he seems to sway briefly into himself, delivering what have often after the fact been quoted as his friend's final words to the world: *Music has given me over forty years of extraordinary experiences. I can't say that life's pains or more tragic episodes have been diminished because of it, but it has allowed me so many moments of companionship when I have been lonely, and a sublime means of communication when I have wanted to touch people. It has been both my doorway of perception and the house that I live in.*

The nightly news omits asking who Oldman's speechwriter might have been and why he didn't know those weren't really Bowie's last words to the world.

It fails to point out that the passage Oldman quotes is in reality part of a commencement speech Bowie delivered seventeen years earlier at Berklee College, a private music school in Boston known for its studies in jazz, hip-hop, reggae, salsa, heavy metal, and bluegrass.

It misses the fact that Oldman leaves out the final two sentences from that speech—*I only hope that [music] embraces you with the same lusty life force it graciously offered me. Thank you very much, and remember: If it itches, play it*—followed by the pensive, puzzled silence on the young spectators' part before comprehending it was time to applaud, which they do, noticeably, with less than one hundred percent conviction.

## ALWAYS CRASHING IN THE SAME CAR (II)

The nightly news does not comment on how David Bowie's breathing became increasingly shallow and ragged on the morning of January 10, 2016 as he whirled through his morphine journey, a signal to Iman that it was, after a long, hard night, time to call in Lexi, Duncan, and Coco, who had been keeping each other company, dozing on and off in the living room.

It does not show Bowie's wife, daughter, son, and confidant entering and taking their places around his hospital bed, laying hands upon the singer in a bid to ease his departure.

It does not record Bowie's real last words to the world, which comprised a few garbled half-syllables originating from deep inside his delusions and oxygen starvation.

How Lexi is certain she heard her father say: *Some sentence is always the last.*

While to Duncan the noises sounded like: *What could possibly come next?*

And Coco will always swear she could make out a question in there: *Did you hear what I just said?*

Iman, however, will believe to her own last breath that she was the only one to hear her husband's terminal utterance clearly, and it was this: *Come back. Come back. Come back.*

Nor does the nightly news note that none of those in attendance was correct.

## ACKNOWLEDGMENTS

Although *Always Crashing in the Same Car* involved extensive research and deals with historical events and individuals, it is a novel through and through and should be taken as such. In other words, while real persons, both alive and deceased, are depicted in its pages, their actions, motivations, and conversations are wholly fictitious. Rather, this book aims to be an exploration into the problematics of pastness, into how all biographies, all the spiritual autobiographies we call criticism, are, in a sense, exercises in beautiful futility. I couldn't have created what appears here without imagining through the work of many others, among the most important of which—besides the whole of David Bowie's music, to which I listened continuously while composing this book—proved to be: Sonia Anderson's *Bowie: The Man Who Changed the World*, David Buckley's *Strange Fascination: Bowie: The Definitive Story*, Dylan Jones's *David Bowie: The Oral History*, Wendy Leigh's *Bowie: The Biography*, Alec Lindsell's *The Sacred Triangle: Bowie, Iggy & Lou 1971–1973*, John O'Connell's *Bowie's Bookshelf: The Hundred Books That Changed David Bowie's Life*, Francis Whately's *David Bowie: The Last Five Years*; the conversations collected in *David Bowie: The Last Interview and Other Conversations;* the

*David Bowie Is* . . . exhibition, as it appeared in Berlin in 2014; and *David Bowie: Critical Perspectives* (edited by Eoin Devereux, Aileen Dillane, and Martin J. Power). Many thanks to *Big Other, Black Scat Review, Gobshite Quarterly, manuskripte, Stat®Rec* and Anti-Oedipus Press for publishing excerpts from *Always Crashing,* and to The Rockefeller Foundation Bellagio Center, at which I was able to complete my work on the manuscript.